Nothing Remains the Same

NOTHING REMAINS THE SAME

Meeka O'Brien

TENTH STREET PRESS

THIS EDITION

Published by Tenth Street Press   2013
Revised January 2014

Cover design courtesy of Tenth Street Press

ISBN10: 0-9876027-0-5

ISBN13: 978-0-9876027-0-1

National Library of Australia Cataloguing-in-Publication entry

Author: O'Brien, Meeka, author.

Title: Nothing remains the same / Meeka O'Brien.

ISBN: 9780987602701 (paperback)

Dewey Number: A823.4

Also available in digital formats
ISBN13: 978-0-9874399-9-4

PRINTED IN THE U.S.A.

TENTH STREET PRESS Ltd.
MELBOURNE LONDON
contact@tenthstreetpress.com
www.tenthstreetpress.com

Dedication

I dedicate this book to each and every one who has touched my life

Neil who fills my life with love and light

Niek for his powerful messages

You all came to me with a gift in your hands.

Thank you!

CONTENTS

Chapter 1
The ray of the Sun and the ray of the Moon

Lindiwi holds her breath when another strong pain builds up inside her. It intensifies and she feels as if it is ripping her whole body apart. With a quick movement she wipes away the tears that are forcing themselves through her clenched eyelids. She bites down hard on her teeth and gives the two midwifes, who seem to be unconcerned, a nervous glance. She doesn't want to make a sound, not even a whimper.

The pain slowly begins to fade and she makes an effort to control her ragged breathing. She jerks with fright when a crested barbet lets out a long, sustained trilling "Trrrrrrrr." The loud sound rings in her ears and she feels as if the bird is making an urgent announcement that her life is to be changed forever.

A smouldering fire in the centre of the partly smoked filled hut, adds more heat to the already unbearable hot temperature. Yesterday she still found pleasure in decorating the outside walls with bright colours. She still had the energy to keep the inside tidy and each object placed neatly, elegantly and thoughtfully.

She is unable to keep her hands still and runs her trembling fingers along the wide black stripe on the back of a soft ginger jackal skin. The hut that yesterday was a safe and welcome haven now feels oppressive, harsh and suffocating. She swallows hard to stop the burning dry sensation in her throat. Her hands flutter up to her short, curly black hair and she gives a sigh when she feels it is wet and dishevelled. She likes to keep it neat and tidy. Even her smooth, bulging stomach shines as if it has been rubbed with oil. She sneaks a quick look at the two midwives, who are sitting close to the open entrance chatting and drinking sour milk. A light, listless wind flutters around them reflecting her mood.

In secret she has made many offerings to the Great Spirit to insure she will give birth to a boy. Her strained lips soften and her big brown eyes widen while a tiny giggle bubbles through her at the thought. Outside the crested barbet gives another long, trilling "Trrrrrrr." This time it doesn't startle her, instead the thought crosses her mind that he could be declaring to the world she is about to give birth to a boy. Her soft mouth pulls in a stubborn line. It is going to be perfect! It is not her fault his other wives could not produce a son. She will be the one to give him an heir!

She is forced back to reality when another contraction begins. She waits in anticipation for its full force. This is her first child and her husband's other wives told her that giving birth would be no worse than a bad stomach cramp. They lied! This is a difficult, slow and painful process. A small groan escapes and she tries to stop it by holding her hand over her mouth. She fights the pain, but at the same time, she is learning that nature will complete the birthing cycle in its own time, no matter how long it takes or how painful the process.

The older midwife glances at her sharply, then turns to her younger assistant and tells her to start preparing an herbal mixture to relieve Lindiwi's pain. She clicks her tongue at the restless girl behind her but makes no effort to get up. She is aware that Lindiwi is frightened and feels alone, but her pride won't allow her to give any comfort. She lifts her head and stares outside with cold eyes. Lindiwi is a descendant of Nzunza and she and the other villagers' descendants of Manala! Who can forget the deceit of the Nzunza people and the treachery against King Musi?

The cold look sends a shiver down Lindiwi's spine. It has been obvious from the day she arrived at the village that she was not accepted. Subservient to the First Wife she tried to fulfil her allotted tasks as best she could, but nothing she did really mattered. Nothing could exclude her from the weaving thread of mistrust and jealousy.

The younger midwife mixes the crushed herbs with some warm water. She is almost a younger version of the older midwife. Already her body is showing signs of becoming plump and her face has the same roundness. She avoids looking at Lindiwi, afraid that the older midwife, who is her teacher, might see compassion in her eyes. The envious glances, mistrust and loneliness must have been hard for Lindiwi. Even when Lindiwi's graceful walk, accentuating her wide swinging hips, became slow and impeded with her bulging stomach, she was constantly observed.

She walks over to Lindiwi and hands her the herbal mixture. Lindiwi hesitates and she encourages in a low voice. "Drink, it will help for the pain." She avoids eye contact with Lindiwi and suppresses an impulse to comfort her. Without waiting to see if Lindiwi drinks the mixture she gets up and moves away. Her eyes dash to the older midwife. She is still in training and won't do anything to jeopardize it. She sits down and even with her limited experience she knows it won't be long now.

Lindiwi swallows the herbal mixture quickly with shaking hands. It is bitter and revolting. The taste rises up from her burning stomach and she has to swallow hard to stop herself from vomiting. At almost the same instant her stomach tightens with another contraction. It builds and intensifies until a needle sharp pain follows a movement in her lower abdomen.

Like the slow unstoppable movement of the rising sun, pain is following the same cycle. Nothing can stop the red-hot rays of the sun from creating a new day. It will only lose its strength when the day is done. Then, and only then, the temperature will become more bearable. The rays of the sun will turn soft and gentle and a cool light wind, will apologize for the intense heat.

The midwives bustle around Lindiwi with more urgency now. They have been with her since early morning and judging by the intensity and length of the contractions, it won't be long now.

Lindiwi gives another hard and painful push and feels the baby slide out of her wet, perspiring and tired body. She lets out a long sigh of relief and relaxes. At the same time the sun is slowly starting to creep away behind the horizon but she doesn't notice. Her only concern right now is to look at her newborn child.

The eagerness and anticipation leaves her in an instant when another pain shoots like a knife stab through her body. She screams in alarm and grabs the hand of the younger midwife. Her eyes beg for help between her alarm and confusion.

The younger midwife is as surprised as Lindiwi and looks at the older midwife with an unspoken question in her eyes. The older midwife ignores both her trainee and the frightened young mother. She keeps her eyes downcast and pretends to search for more firewood. She does this because she wants to hide from them the age-old knowledge of experience.

While the sunlight outside makes way for the soft glow of the moon, the birthing process that Lindiwi thought was completed, starts all over again. Another herbal concoction is shoved unceremoniously in her hand. It is stronger than the previous brew and even though the bitter, vile taste burns her mouth she seems unaware of it. Everything has lost its meaning except the red-hot fierce pain tormenting her. While the moon slowly rises higher in the sky, Lindiwi gives birth to a second child.

Drained from the infants, that had sucked almost the last drops of life from her, she closes her eyes wearily. Nothing matters much at the moment, whether it is day or night, warm or cold. The darkness of exhaustion enfolds her and she embraces it. She knows the midwives will take care of the two children she has just born.

Outside the moon continues its movement. It doesn't have the harsh heat of the sun and appears to bring a cool, calming effect upon the earth. However, those who have taken the time to watch and learn know it is only an illusion. They know that while the moon fulfils its task of creating night, just as the sun created day, other forces are at work.

While everyone sleeps under the seemingly soft and gentle rays of the moon, the Spirit People awaken. This is their time! It is the time when the ancestors wake up and come and visit their families. They sometimes talk and advise you through dreams and visions and if you are lucky, some predictions. Yes, the moon time can be strange and scary!

The Spirit People, hidden in the darkness, look at the two children born from the same womb. It is like the cycle of the seasons, spring and summer, autumn and winter, the rotation of the universe is steady, continuous and unstoppable.

In the distance a lion roars and the Spirit People begin to dance. Thukani will be here soon..........

Thukani is rushing home. He has just received news that Lindiwi has started her birthing process. He is about one day's walk from home as their hunting expedition had taken them further than what he originally intended. To make matters worse, his best and life long friend Bongwe slipped and fell down a sharp ravine breaking his arm.

As soon as his First Wife's messenger found them, he left the slow moving group behind and rushed ahead. While departing hurriedly he heard Bongwe making jokes about his own misfortune. Bongwe is such a jovial fellow, always laughing and making jokes. Thukani gives a rare smile. His white teeth sparkle momentarily in sharp contrast to his darker skin. He is tall and well built, attractive in spite of his slightly hooked nose.

He has deep feelings for Bongwe, the only person he has ever allowed himself to develop a close friendship with. He realizes that he sometimes needs the light-hearted Bongwe to take his mind off the serious matters that he has to deal with.

As the territorial chief and direct descendant of Manala, he needs to make serious decisions that could affect them all. Squabbling and strife between neighbours and families take up a lot of his time. It is up to him to make a final decision that will settle the argument. Sometimes he needs to keep his cool and direct his warriors to track and destroy vagabonds and nomads that try to steal their cattle. His responsibilities sometimes feel overwhelming but he keeps at it with persistence and determination.

He hesitated to go on the hunting expedition but Bongwe convinced him that it will be good for him to hunt instead of sitting around waiting for Lindiwi to give birth. Luck could be on their side and they could find a wildebeest, an animal with lots of meat and a strong skin. He increases his pace and relies on his accompanying warriors to look out for lions that might attack them. Lions are difficult to see as they hide in the long grass, barely visible to the human eye.

Some of the warriors stayed behind to help Bongwe. It is always an advantage to help the trusted and best friend of the leader. Maybe someday the favour could be returned!

Thukani's athletic body is soaking wet from the fast pace he is maintaining. Some of his warriors do their utmost to hide the fact that they would love to just rest awhile, maybe in the cooling shade of a big tree. They've been walking for hours without rest, but none of them will dare complain. It could cost them dearly should they do so! Thukani's temper is not something one would willingly test.

As they are close enough to reach the village easily before the darkness of night, Thukani gestures to his men to take a break. Grateful the men sag down to embrace the cool shade of an old jacaranda tree.

Smangaliso, the head warrior, hands Thukani a calabash filled with cool water to quench his thirst. He drinks fast and deep then gives the empty calabash back to Smangaliso without a word of thanks.

Thoughts spin around in his head. Did Lindiwi give birth to a son or will he be cursed with yet another daughter. His teeth grind in frustration and he grumbles under his breath. "All girls! How on earth can I hand over the leadership of my people to a woman?" His frustrated fingers scratches through his short curly black hair and his frown deepens. Even Bongwe constantly jokes about how colourful all his huts will be painted by his many daughters. He gets up and starts walking again. Too much time has already passed!

It is just after midday when they enter the village. Heat waves rise up from the hot earth and cling to the approaching men's bodies, giving them a ghost like, shimmering appearance.

Thukani frowns as he notices that people hurry and scuttle to their huts as if they are trying to avoid him. It makes him feel decidedly uncomfortable and unwillingly his stomach tightens with tension and an unexpected feeling of doom.

He heads towards Lindiwi's hut with long strides. At the hut he doesn't bother to knock or ask permission to enter, as is the custom. He simply walks inside rudely.

Surprised by his unexpected entrance the two midwifes jump up. They bow their heads in respect. They are tense and nervous in his presence and when he ignores them and heads towards Lindiwi, they scamper out the door as quickly as they can. They have no intention of sticking around to see Thukani's reaction. Thukani is also known as "Isilwane," which means lion, and everyone knows it is dangerous to be on the wrong side of a lion.

Without bothering to ask about Lindiwi's welfare he focuses on the small covered bundle beside her. "Well, what is it!" he barks in a gruff voice.

Lindiwi suppresses her weariness and struggles to sit upright. Her brown eyes appear bigger than usual in her pinched face. She tries to combat her nervousness by patting her hair with shaking fingers. She swallows hard and clears her throat but can only utter a hoarse, nervous croak. "It is a boy my husband."

Thukani's face breaks into a wide, delightful and rare smile. He hurries forward, kneels next to her and jerks the blanket off the infant. When he sees the two little boys instead of the one he expected, he jumps up with shock and his smile disappears in the same instant. He wipes his hands on his legs with disgust as if he has just touched something vile and rotten. He is not impressed to see twins!

Lindiwi utters a low anguished groan and sinks down on the mat. She grabs the soft, colourful woven baby blanket and covers her head in shame. Under the almost comforting and near darkness of the blanket, she bites her already tight lips to stop the sobs rising within her. She has been dreading the moment of his arrival and now that he is here, it is even worse than what she had anticipated.

Thukani looks at her covered head with cold eyes. He hears her soft cries but doesn't speak any words of comfort or otherwise to her. His stomach and fists are clenched in anger. He wants to scream and shout at the injustice! He feels as if a kudu had just pierced him with its exotic horns. Sharp and smooth, like butter melting on hot cornmeal.

Disgusted he swings around and storms out of the hut. He cannot, and nor will he, accept either of the boys until it has been decided whether one or neither of the boys can be his rightful heir. According to their teachings, two children born at the same time, from the same womb, indicates evil forces at work.

Some people even went as far as to say that it is only one soul born with two bodies, one containing the good part and the other the evil part. Therefore when a woman bore two children at the same time, one of them had to be destroyed. Only then will the chosen one have the full opportunity to live a happy life without evil influences. Sometimes it could even be necessary to destroy both children, especially if it cannot be determined who is the chosen one.

Lindiwi hears her husband leave and the tears break through the floodgates of her strained emotions. She harshly criticizes herself. "I have failed him! I have failed my husband!" All her meticulous plans were for nothing. When one of the boys starts crying she takes the blanket off her tearstained face. She picks him up and puts him to her breast so he can suckle.

The two midwives enter the hut and look at her in shocked silence. Surely she knows she shouldn't feed the infants till a final decision has been made?

With an undeniable challenge in her eyes, Lindiwi defies them. "Try and stop me!" she says, without uttering a word. She will allow the other one to suckle as well.

In silence the two midwives turns around and pretend to busy themselves with the dishes. They can hear Thukani's loud call to his head warrior Smangaliso outside.

"Tell the elders I want a meeting!" Thukani orders. "Make sure they understand that it is urgent and come straight away. I have no intention of waiting for them to scuffle along and only get here after sunset. Now go!"

Smangaliso calmly nods his head and calls some of his most trusted warriors in his low, slow voice. He is a large rock of a man with a big, clean-shaven head, fairly large nose and heavy jaw. His warriors listen intently to his instructions. They know he will not repeat them. They run in different directions and Smangaliso watches them go. His eyes are carefully veiled so no distinct expression is visible.

Thukani briskly walks out of the village to the nearby river. He notices nothing around him. He just wants to be alone. He wants to gather his thoughts and try and find some sense in what had happened.

"Why did it have to be twins?" he grunts. "If I loose both boys, I'll have no heir. If one is to be disposed off which one should it be?" Frustrated he kicks at a loose rock under his feet and wishes for a moment the insouciant Bongwe was with him to lighten the heavy load.

He swings around when he hears the trilling "Trrrrrrrrrr," of a barbet. It reminds him of the strange dream he had two nights ago. In his dream he is walking in the bright sunlight and sees a crested barbet with an orange face and erectile shaggy chest. The barbet puffs his chest and displays his yellow under parts and broad black band. In its beak it has a green twig with red berries on it.

The barbet flies closer to him. It flutters around his left ear, then moves to the other side and flutters around his right ear. It annoys and irritates him! He tries to swipe it away, but the nimble bird avoids his blows with ease. Suddenly the barbet bites down hard on the twig and it breaks in two.

One piece falls on his shoulder and he grabs it. He swears under his breath when he feels a sharp pain. He looks at his hand and notices blood dripping from a deep pinprick. His eyes widen in surprise. He didn't realize there were sharp thorns hidden between the berries.

For some strange and unknown reason he takes one of the berries and puts it in his mouth. It is bitter and burns like red-hot coals. With disgust he spits it out but the bitter, burning taste lingers.

The crested barbet lets out another long, trilling "Trrrrrr," swoops down, picks up the other half of the twig that fell to the ground, and flies away.

He tries to rid himself of the oppressive feeling the dream brings by throwing a stone into the water. It doesn't seem to work and he turns on his heels and walks to a nearby ridge. He climbs it as fast as he can and the strenuous exercise relieves some of the tension.

He can see the village nestled in the bottom of the valley. It looks calm and tranquil. Children shriek in high-excited voices and working woman chatter with busy hands. Huts with bright, elaborate geometrical patterns add beauty to an already green and lush countryside. He can see some of the older girls helping their mothers paint and decorate the huts. Bright and intricate patterns form and flow from their hands. He will stay here as long as he can.

Chapter 2
The Wisdom of the Elders

Situated on the east side of the village, where the sun rises, is a round cleared circle. The outside of the fairly large clearing is fenced off with long wooden branches. The wood has long since dried from the harshness of the sun and combined with the forces of the wind, they are now smooth and white. Inside on wooden seats, as white and smooth as the fence, all placed together, some of the selected elders have already gathered. Their mood is serious, almost sombre. Not all elders are automatically selected to attend meetings regarding important matters. The right to attend has to be earned.

Thukani is on his way to the meeting. He paces himself so he does not walk too fast. He notices some anxious mothers collecting their children and disappearing into their huts. He is aware that some of the young adults glance longingly towards the meeting place. They would love to attend! Usually it would mildly amuse him but today he ignores it, forgetting that he once gazed at the meeting place with the same ache in his heart.

He waits at the entrance. He cannot enter until all the elders are seated and comfortable. To do so would be rude and disrespectful, something he cannot afford to do at this stage. His body is tense while he paces backwards and forwards. Part of him wants to pick up their slow moving bodies and hurry them along, while another part of him dreads this meeting.

It is almost a humiliating time for him. As territorial chief he has the power to make any decision. It will be final and no one will dare disobey. The matter of his heir however, is one decision he cannot make on his own. For his heir to be accepted into the community, the boy has to be approved and accepted by the chosen elders as well. In this way it is insured that the rightful heir is not deviously replaced with another.

He shakes his head. Sometimes their customs frustrate him, but his strong cultural upbringing stops him from even mentioning it. As chief he understands too well the value of rules. Reluctantly he recalls the pompous way he summoned the elders. A nagging little stab also reminds him that some of the elders have not been pleased with decisions he had made in the past. It could become a day where old scores are settled. Today they hold the spear of life and death in their wrinkled hands. Tension weaves its thread even tighter around him. It is suffocating and he hates it!

Through an opening in the fence Thukani's oldest daughter Sibongile is watching. She is not allowed to be anywhere near the meeting place. She is taller than all the other 13-year-old teenagers in the village and already has an aura of authority about her. She has inherited her father's hooked nose, though it is not so pronounced. Added to her high cheekbones and fine features it adds to her attractiveness.

Normally she is very obedient and would never disobey her parents, and acting on impulse is not in her nature. However her desire to watch was so overwhelming and strong, that she carefully made plans and chose a good hiding place. The moment the opportunity arose she sneaked away and settled to watch the proceedings.

At long last everyone is settled and Thukani enters. He intercepts Nomsa's cold and piercing look. Her old body is thin and bony and her head is covered with a ragged and dirty head cloth. She gives him a toothless smile that looks more like a grin. It doesn't reach her dark, beady eyes. He looks away making no effort to cover his disgust and she gives a high-pitch penetrating laugh at his reaction. "The old hag," he thinks, "she probably already knows that Lindiwi gave birth to twins."

Nomsa never accepted that Thukani didn't want to marry her daughter. In fact she was downright offended by it. She hates his proud and arrogant look and her beady eyes, set deep in her skull, glint with dark hatred. He betrayed her and her tribe in more ways than one.

Thukani takes his place in front of the elders. Silently they wait for him to speak. He pulls his tall, well built, athletic body upright and lifts his head proudly. His whole stature says." You might hold the spear of life and death in your hands today, but I am Chief Thukani! I am the brave and proud warrior known as Isilwane, the Lion!"

Some of the women sigh deeply as they see the tight muscles in his arms and chest. It forms an amazing picture of virility and strength. The soft impala skin around his waist completes the vision of his majesty. Some have a colder more calculating look in their eyes, especially the ones who had to deal with his ruthlessness and stubbornness sometime or another.

Satisfied that he has achieved exactly the effect he was aiming for he lifts his spear high and cries. "The Ndebele People have always been strong and brave! Others look upon us with fear and envy. You only need to look at our warriors and cattle grazing in the field, to see how strong and powerful we have become. We stand tall and proud! We are the Ndebele People!"

The elders nod their heads and their chest swell with pride. It is important that they stay strong. The anticipation of Lindiwi producing an heir to Thukani has been intense.

Thukani nods to Smangaliso to fetch the infants. He feels better now that he has seen the effect of his words on the elders.

Smangaliso acknowledges by bowing his large head. He walks with slow secure steps over to Lindiwi's hut. He calls out and once permission is given, enters. He leaves the hut with two small covered bundles and returns to the waiting elders. When he enters and the elders see that he has two bundles instead of the expected one, they let out a loud gasp and eyes fly open in horror. He places the two infants, who are hardly bigger than his huge hands carefully on a bright coloured woven mat. His face is expressionless.

Thukani ignores the elders' reaction. "Sometimes the Great Spirit gives us trials and tribulations. It serves to make us strong and teach us valuable lessons. We have no control over such things, just as I had no control over Lindiwi giving birth to two boys. However, we must accept the Great Spirit's wisdom just as we accept that we are the first he created.

The Great Spirit also knows that for the Ndebele people to continue to be strong and powerful, they need a strong and wise leader. Look at the baboons. Even they have a leader. Without a leader to guide them there would be chaos in the ranks and no order in their daily tasks. The leader is the one who knows where there is enough food and where they will be safe from the crushing jaws of the crocodile.

He shows the young how to be brave and strong. When the powerful baboon leader stands erect and bares his teeth, many tremble, for they know the strength that is hidden beneath his hairy body. They know that he can tear a man in apart with his powerful arms. They know that the appearance he presents, when he sits peacefully in the sun scratching his stomach, is nothing compared to what he can become when his troops are in danger. His strength makes him a formidable fighter striving to keep his troops safe and secure. Yes, even the baboon knows that for their fundamental survival, they need a strong leader!"

Everyone is carried along like a flowing river with the passion in his voice and he uses it to his full advantage. "The Great Spirit has left it up to you, respected elders, to decide who the next chief will be. He expects you to choose wisely. He knows the future of a strong Ndebele nation depends on it!"

Aware that the elders might not accept either of the boys he had chosen his words with care. He wants them to think that the idea didn't even occur to him. He turns and nods to Smangaliso again and the head warrior steps forward and opens the two covered bundles.

Both infants start crying. Their arms swing desperately for the comfort of their mother and their thin and tiny legs kick high with fear. Their small fearful cries combine and wail a chorus of desperation.

The elders stare at the two infants. Their cries unwillingly pulls Thukani's gaze as well. His head jerks up and his eyes flash darkly when he hears Nomsa's loud, cold-hearted and pretended whisper to Nyathela. "I'm glad the screaming whelps aren't part of my family!"

He forces himself to remain calm but a fierce fire has burned a mark of doom for Nomsa in his heart. Instead he tries to determine what the elders are thinking. All they seem to be doing is staring stupidly at the infants. His fists clench from all the tension inside him as he keeps his piercing look on the elders. He shuts his ears to the infants desperate howling. He doesn't want to look at them!

Nyathela, a very old and respected elder struggles to her feet. It is a slow and painful process for her. Slowly she shuffles towards the twins. Her shoulders are hunched and she leans onto a walking stick for support with claw-like hands. Her small, yet bright eyes in her wrinkled and age old face peers at the infants. Her failing eyesight forces her to shuffle even closer. Her intuition is sending her signals that there is something important she needs to see. Wisps of grey hair flutter in the wind. She screeches and points to one of the boys.

All eyes have been on Nyathela and they strain to see what she is pointing at. Her opinion is considered very valuable.

Nomsa jumps up and shatters the silence with her own high-excited squeal. She rushes forward and grabs the smaller boy hard handily with her bony and dirty hands. She lifts him high into the air while pointing at his hip.

The infant cries out. His little arms and legs flutter helplessly as this harsh and unknown terror enfolds him. On his hip there is a dapple, a small gleaming white mark in the shape of a triangle.

The elders gasp! A black child with a white mark, surely there is something sinister about that?

Thukani sees the perfect white triangle on his son's hip. A shiver runs with icy cold fierceness up and down his back. The triangle seems to have a bright luminous glow and he glances around quickly, almost nervously. He is not sure if he is the only one perceiving it in this way. He forces himself to look away and clench his fists for the umpteenth time today. He will not allow a simple triangle to affect him!

The tension is broken when Nyathela calls for the two midwives that were present during the birth. After a while of intense questioning it is clear that the first and bigger boy was born under the rays of the sun, while the smaller boy was born under the rays of the moon. This information is of vital importance to Nyathela because of the sinister forces at play during the darkness of the moon.

She points to the smaller boy and addresses the gathering in her quivering voice. "This child was born under the rule of the moon. He has a strange mark on his hip. It is an evil mark that he tried to conceal by entering the world under the cover of darkness. He was born second indicating that he was not the first choice of the Great Spirit." She spits on the ground to show her disgust. "I suggest we dispose of him immediately, preferably before night falls and he harms the rightful heir to Thukani."

The elders nod their heads in agreement. The child with the evil mark will be disposed off without any further deliberation. The other child will be accepted and acknowledged as Thukani's rightful heir and chief. There is also an air of relief around the elders. Is it not easier to follow the river than swim against it?

Sibongile, hearing the outcome, gives a small cry from her hiding place. Some of the nearby elders glance in her direction and she puts her slender hand in front of her mouth. She squeezes her eyes to stop the flow of tears and sinks down into a small ball. With her arms wrapped around her legs and her head hidden on her knees, she experiences the intensity of a full-blown anger for the first time in her young life.

She too had been fascinated by the triangle on her half brother's hip, but that doesn't mean she wants him dead. Stupid elders, what do they know. She creeps away. She can't bear to watch anymore.

Thukani doesn't challenge the outcome, even though it is within his right to do so. All he is concerned about right now is that one of his sons will survive. He needs an heir and if it takes all his control, pride, and self-indulgence to achieve it, so be it!

He bends down and picks up the marked child. As the father, it is his duty to offer the child to the great crocodile. Without bothering to inform Lindiwi or giving her a chance to say farewell, he heads towards the nearby river. It will make no difference anyhow. The decision has been made.

At the river's edge he lays the boy, who has now stopped crying, down on some soft grass. For a moment his looks down on the small child, then turns around and walks away. One child has to die to fulfil the destiny of the other. That is the way of life. In the muddy waters behind him a crocodile waits. It is almost completely submerged, its protruding nostrils, eyes and a portion of its back are the only visible parts.

Once back in the village he heads to Lindiwi's hut. He calls out asking permission to enter and when she replies he enters. She is nursing their remaining son and her tearstained face pulls at his guilty heartstrings.

She continues to feed the baby as if he isn't there. He kneels next to her and touches her hand to comfort her. With a cold stare she jerks it away. A part of her has died. What does he care that something has been viciously torn from her body in more ways than one. All he wants is an heir!

Stinging from her rejection he says in a tight voice, "My son will be called Matsisi. It is a Manala family name," he adds with a bit of spite.

She continues to ignore him, showing no indication that she had heard what he said. She doesn't care and she will never care again, not for him or anybody else. Her heart is broken and she is broken.

Thukani shrugs his shoulders, gets up and walks out of the hut. Outside he takes a deep breath. The atmosphere inside is too hot and oppressive.

In a nearby hut Sibongile is helping her mother prepare for the big feast and celebrations later that night. Her hands work nimbly but her heart is heavy. She feels like she is carrying a burden. She wishes she had someone to talk to. How is it that no one can see the similarity between the feud of the brothers Manala and Nzunza and what happened tonight?

All children are told the story of King Musi. It is important that all know how Nzunza deceived the old and dying King Musi so that he could become King instead of his older brother Manala. When Manala found out about the deceit he declared war on his brother. This caused a great split in the Ndebele People.

Eventually a peace agreement was made to stop the bloodshed. Both brothers agreed to marry each other's daughter and make her his First Wife. Manala kept his part of the bargain but Nzunza, even though he married his brother's daughter, refused to make her his First Wife. His people refused to honour a girl from the Manala people.

Manala declared war on his brother once more and Nzunza and his followers fled. Broken and homeless they wandered far and wide till they found grace with strangers further north and settled in their valley.

It was purely by accident that Thukani discovered the attractive Lindiwi. She was on her way to attend a wedding of a relative and one of their travelling companions got sick. Their journey had also taken them longer than what they had anticipated and they needed fresh food supplies and medicine. A nearby village seemed the logical place to go. The same village Thukani was visiting to discuss some business matters.

Thukani knew straight away that the young and beautiful Lindiwi is the fresh blood he needed to produce an heir. Lindiwi didn't care that Thukani was part of the Manala people either. She was unmistakably in love with the proud and strong warrior chief. Amidst objections from both sides, he took her home and married her.

Sibongile suspects her father did so because his other wives, including her mother, only gave him daughters. Why would he otherwise choose a wife from the Nzunza people? Again she wishes with all her heart that she had someone to talk to. It seems that no one considers all the facts. Lindiwi is a descendant of Nzunza. Thukani is a descendant of Manala. The child they have just killed has the blood of King Musi running in his veins!

Chapter 3

The Universe Conspires

The sun has almost completed its cycle and the moon is already visible in the sky. It becomes the magical and mystical time when day and night meet. It is also a strange time when strange things can happen. In the river the water continues to bubble and splatter over rocks. Outwardly it looks like all things remain the same, but it is only an illusion.

In between the bushes hides a woman. She has been there since mid afternoon to wait for the arrival of the child. She is alert and pays attention to every movement around her. Timing is very important and the window of opportunity is very small.

Last night she could feel the excitement and joy of the Spirit People and she now feels the same excitement stir in her chest. At long last, everything they have been waiting for, for what seems an eternity, is becoming a reality.

Mthisa is a small, dark and rather fierce looking woman. Her eyes are sharp and penetrating and dominate her whole face. A faded head cloth that is tied at the back, also serving to keep her hair out of her face, covers her long black hair. Her clothes, though clean, have seen their best days, but she wears them with confidence. She really couldn't be bothered with something as trivial as her appearance.

She is just about to crawl out of her hiding place when she hears the sound of excited voices. It is a group of young men. They are still children, yet already crossing the thin and difficult line to adulthood.

They spur and prompt each in excited, yet half fearful, voices to the river's edge.

Mthisa feels like screaming. She doesn't have a lot of time and now she has to deal with the inquisitive, trying to act brave but are not, irritating boys. Her eagle sharp glare doesn't leave them for a moment. She clicks her tongue and wishes she could get up from her hiding place and scare the little bit of daylight that is left out of them. "What's wrong with the young people of today? How can they find pleasure in such a gruesome act?"

The boys come to a sudden halt when they see a crocodile swimming in the water with rhythmic strokes of its tail. They scamper away from the river's edge and almost stumble upon another crocodile basking in the last rays of the weak afternoon sun. It makes a hissing sound and opens its mouth to reveal vicious looking teeth. It could be a female protecting her eggs!

As fast as they can, they run to a safe distance. Fast glances scan in all directions in case a crocodile is heading towards them in a quick belly crawl. All they want to see is how the crocodile rotates rapidly before tearing his prey apart. They don't want to become a meal!

Mthisa is still keeping a sharp eye on the boys when the infant starts crying. She grinds her teeth. His wails will attract all kinds of scavengers. She slowly pushes the branches of the bush away and looks around. It could be that she can grab the baby before the boys notice. She shakes her head. The moment she leaves her hiding place the boys will see her, something she cannot afford to happen.

Carefully she slips the branches, obstructing her from the boys view, back into place. She doesn't waste anymore time. Danger is moving closer to the precious little boy. She needs help and she needs it fast.

She closes her eyes and makes a conscious effort to relax. She takes deep rhythmic breaths and starts rocking backwards and forwards as much as she can, without disclosing her hiding place. Her thoughts are closed to time and space. It is the only way to connect to the Spirit People. Hardly audible, with her head bowed, she starts chanting in a strange and mystical language.

She continues to rock and chant, rock and chant, till her eyes lose their vision and everything around her becomes cloudy and hazy. Unaware of anything around her, she has moved into what is known to her as the Spirit World. It is the place where the Spirit People and the ancestors live. It is also the home of the Great Spirit from where he rules the world and everything in it.

She knows that from this special place, she can communicate with every living thing on earth and beyond. Here it doesn't matter whether you are man or woman, animal or plant. Here everyone and everything is the same. There are no barriers, not even that of language or tradition. Everyone allowed to be in this place knows that it is the safest place on earth.

Her body stops moving and becomes nothing. All she is with at the moment is her mind:

I call to the Guardians of the Watchtower of the East where all days are born. You are yellow like the sun and have the power to make things grow.

I call to the Guardians of the Watchtower of the South. You are red hot like the fire. Your energy gives us our blood red life force.

I call to the Guardians of the Watchtower of the West. You are blue like the sky and water. You are tranquil and calm and contain all the wisdom.

I call to the Guardians of the Watchtower of the North. You are black like the night and your darkness has the power to kill.

Be here with me now Guardians!

Great Spirit I stand small and humble in your great and infinite presence. Everything is You, Great Spirit, and I see only You in all things. Your Divine Spirit surrounds me and is within me, always. I know that this is not for me alone, but for all Your children. I know that I have nothing that they do not have. The Great Spirit is for all!

Be here with me now Great Spirit!

Spirit People wake up and help me. Merge yourself in me so that we can become one and I can be united with your power.

Be here with me now Spirit People!

I am Mthisa, forever your servant. I am of the trees and of the fields. I am of the streams and the hills. I am part of you, just as you are part of me. The beloved child is in danger. Please help me save him.

Her small body shivers like a leaf clinging precariously against a strong wind. "Hurry!" she pleads. "Please hurry!" Her body is still and calm and the only sensation she feels is the familiar pulling sensation in the centre of her forehead. The Spirit People are here.

A sudden jerk in her body brings her back to the present and her surroundings. She takes a deep breath. All has been said, there is nothing more she can do but wait. There is no doubt in her mind that her request was answered. That is one of the first things the Spirit People taught her. When you have asked for something, know that it is done. Don't go back to the asking again, it implies doubt.

The group of young boys stops their excited chatter when an elephant trumps nearby. When they see a large bull approaching they know it is time to leave. They don't contemplate on whether he has come to feed or indulge in a mud bath. They leave as quickly as they can. They are disappointed, but it gives them some comfort to know a crocodile won't attack while the elephant is there. Maybe they could come back later.

The large elephant bull walks almost noiselessly and with exceptional grace towards the infant. Its large columnar legs keep his bulk moving in smooth, rhythmic strides. He stops dangerously close to the infant and looks down. His eyesight, from his small eyes fixed on his large and relatively immobile head, is poor. With his trunk, his most sensitive organ, he gently touches and smells the now silent infant.

He has moved as close to infant as his large body will allow. He places his feet with care so that he doesn't harm the little one. He has heard the Great Spirit ask them to protect this child and he will do so with his life. His two enormous tusks gleam white and strong and his ears flap around his head cooling him down. Only by looking at his eyes, can you see his apparent quiet stature hides an inner alertness.

Strong and solid, aware of his own strength, it will take a very foolish man or beast to challenge him!

Mthisa crawls out of her hiding place. She mutters under her breath, her legs are stiff and sore from being in a still and cramped position. Intuitively she knows the elephant is there to help her. She doesn't concern herself about the form of the help she is receiving. She has learned that the Spirit People sometimes work in strange ways.

She approaches the elephant carefully with small, slow steps. He watches her but remains still, except for his trunk, which he lifts in the air to pick up her scent. Without any sudden movements she puts her bag on the ground and unties the blanket around her waist.

She bends down and picks up the silent infant. She allows herself only a moment to look at him before she puts him on her back. She covers him with the blanket and ties the ends in front of her body at the top of her breast and then her waist. With the infant secure she retrieves the bag.

She takes out a small calabash filled with blood from a rabbit she had slain earlier and sprinkles it around the area. Every animal within miles will smell the blood and come looking for an easy prey. It will also help cover any signs she may inadvertently have left behind.

She stuffs the empty calabash back into her bag and tilts her head to look at the elephant. The mighty beast towers above her, yet he stands perfectly still, allowing her to do what she must. She wishes with all her heart that she could talk to him and say thank you. With her right hand she touches her forehead, her mouth and her stomach. Then she extends her hand palm up as a gesture of gratitude.

The great one extends his trunk and softly places it in Mthisa's hand. Woman and animal share in that moment perfect love, perfect understanding, and perfect harmony. They are one with each other. Not because of what they did, but because of what they feel.

Birds flutter noisily in a nearby tree as a signal that the moment must end. With one last look at the elephant, Mthisa hurries into the darkness that is descending rapidly now. She fleetingly remembers a vision she had once about a beast similar to an elephant. They were huge gigantic animals with long hair and tusks larger than anything she has ever seen.

The elephant bull flaps his ears to circulate the air and watch her leave. He stays in the same position till the moon is high in the sky. He lifts his head and with his nasal passage produces a low rumbling sound. He is communicating with the herd that he has fulfilled their part.

Under the cover of darkness Mthisa walks, and runs when she can, in her quick moving small steps. It is as if the whole universe has responded to her prayer for help. Thick clouds have moved in to cover the rays of the moon thereby making visibility so poor that Mthisa is barely detectable in the darkness. She knows the area well and moves sure footedly in the direction of her cave. Even though it is a fair distance away, she will not rest until they are both safe.

Just as the moon finished creating the first half of the night, she reaches her cave. She doesn't breathe a sigh of relief until she had secured the branches that cover the entrance. The thick clouds have miraculously disappeared and bright moonbeams illuminate everything in a silver-grey light. Inside Zinhle is waiting for her.

Zinhle helps her untie the infant and hands her something to drink. She makes sure that everything is well with Mthisa and satisfied that it is, she turns her attention to the baby boy. She gets herself comfortable and starts breast-feeding him. Her own little girl is sleeping peacefully beside her. She is big boned and solid. Her face is round with a flat nose, uneven teeth and full lips. She is not very pretty, yet her voice and eyes are soft and gentle while she makes reassuring noises to both babies.

Mthisa lies down beside the flickering fire. She is tired and wishes that she could be alone with her thoughts. She closes her weary eyes. There are only a couple of hours left before they have to leave the protection of the cave and start their long journey.

She opens her eyes again when Zinhle starts singing a soft lullaby. Zinhle doesn't talk much but she can feel that Zinhle knows that they are both fulfilling a destiny. Compassion stirs in her heart for the not so pretty Zinhle, no one deserves to be treated the way she was.

Zinhle was sent, by her family to honour a marriage agreement between two fathers and old friends. She had to travel far, with her new family as companions, to reach the destination where her new husband awaited her. She went willingly, as tradition demanded.

Her new husband however, was not impressed when he saw her. It did not stop him from using her body as often as he could for his own selfish needs, till even that started boring him. It was not long before he accused her of infidelity and his best friend, who had been promised a very lucrative reward, admitted publicly that she seduced him one dark and moonless night.

Ostracized from the village she tried to find her way home, but not knowing the countryside, she soon became lost. Rather than being eaten by predators she decided to take her own life.

Mthisa was gathering herbs when she noticed Zinhle teetering precariously on the edge of a cliff. Instantaneously her senses screamed at her that the woman is important. More than that she could see a small red glow in her belly indicating a new life.

Without Zinhle she would not have been able to complete her mission. Thankful she closes her eyes again and talks softly to herself. "The Spirit People knew when they sent her to me she has a beautiful soul. Maybe one day people will learn that it is not what you look like that is important. When you stand in front of the Great Spirit He doesn't care if you are pretty or ugly. He cares only about what's in your heart.

Irritated Mthisa sits up and throws another stick in the fire. Her thoughts won't allow her to sleep. How she longs for the comfort of the solitude she usually dreams in. She has not been alone for months and it will be quite awhile before she'll be alone again.

Zinhle looks up when she hears the frustrated sigh from Mthisa but doesn't talk. She discovered very quickly that Mthisa finds the company of other people tiresome. One still evening she dared to ask Mthisa about her life and Mthisa explained.

"People don't understand the way I live. They think I am secretive and have things to hide. Some like to call me a hermit, some call me a witchdoctor, and once while collecting herbs I heard strange men from a far off land call me a Sharman. I don't care what they call me," she said and shrugged her shoulders "I know that the food that enters the mind is more important than the food that enters the stomach." She gazed deep into the embers of the fire and continued, "I am never alone. Everything that is, is alive. It doesn't matter where I am, I am always surrounded by life."

Zinhle lies down next to the two infants. How thankful she is towards this small fierce looking woman.

A restless Mthisa also lies down again. She forces herself to relax, there is precious little time left before they have to leave the protection of the cave for the long journey ahead. But thoughts can be persistent and will niggle at the back of your mind until you give them attention. Without wanting or trying she remembers when she had her first dream vision of boy twins being born to Thukani and Lindiwi. One cannot change a dream vision only look upon it. However she knew the consequences of such a birth did not look good for either child.

Soon afterwards the Spirit People came to her. They told her that she would have to take the youngest boy and raise him in their ways. Upset and reluctant she pleaded. "Why do I have to raise the child? I know nothing about children!"

"It makes no difference" the Spirit People would insist, "We will help you."

"Why me then?" Mthisa would moan, "Why me?"

"Because the Great Spirit knows you'll be the most perfect person," was their reply.

The more she resisted, the more they persisted and they argued deep into the night. Eventually she gave in. She realised long ago that whenever you resist something, it would persist. Unless she starts seeing it as a blessing, it will become a curse.

While the flames flicker and splatter at the dry wood, Mthisa eventually falls asleep. A large piece of wood snaps and breaks from the insistent force of the licking flame but she is unaware. At long last her body and mind is resting. Everything has been ready for days. They were simply waiting for the arrival of the boy.

While the Spirit People watch those who live in the world of form, a soft rumble escapes from the earth. It is breathing a deep sigh of relief that the child is safe, at least for tonight. Moonbeams jump with joy between rocks and trees and strange stars shoot across the sky.

The universe is celebrating a beginning! It hopes to change the way people see themselves and, if everything goes according to plan, it will also change the way the people see the Great Spirit.

The Spirit People are excited, yet at the same time apprehensive. They had sent one of their own many years ago to change the people. They had selected one of their most special Spirits and helped him to be reborn as a boy.

At first it seemed as if the people were listening to him and his teachings. Teachings about a beautiful world, a world with no fighting and killing, a world where no one judged another and everyone loved their neighbour as they love themselves. His teachings were spectacular! He showed the people that they were one with the Great Spirit and that the Great Spirit loved them all unconditionally.

How they loved his cheerful and eager soul. They loved the way he used soft and gentle words to try and entice the earth people. Above all, they loved the way he showed them by example, how to live in a way that would gain them entrance to the world he was speaking off. He was willing to risk everything, so that the earth people could discover a world greater than anything they could imagine.

A gust of wind moves a dark cloud in front of the bright moon and the Spirit People stop dancing. They feel sadness well up inside them. They are remembering, how this most special of all souls, was treated. No matter how hard they try, they will never understand. Maybe the people weren't ready to hear his message, or maybe they didn't understand, or maybe they did and refused to change. Who knows? The way of the earth people can sometimes be so unpredictable and fickle.

The Spirit People shiver. The earth people turned on him like savage monsters! They wanted to destroy him! They wanted him dead because his teachings frightened them. They made a cross from wood and planted it in the ground. They tormented and ridiculed him, nailing his body to the ghastly wooden structure so that he could die there!

As if that was not enough, they took his beautiful words and turned and twisted it, like a gnarled old tree, till what was left was just a contorted vision of truth. Like a rock thrown in a pool of still water, the powerful splash created ringed ripples that spread outwards.

Another gust of wind moves the dark cloud away and once again the moon bathes the world in bright moonlight. The mood of the Spirit People lift and they *start dancing again. They jump from moonbeam to moonbeam. A new child is born, and the Great Spirit is going to try again. His plan will unfold slowly, hidden within the unstoppable passage of time.*

Chapter 4
Life Proceeds out of your Intensions for It

Bongwe walks into the village amidst loud celebrations. He had to follow at a slower pace than Thukani, his lifelong friend, because of his broken arm. His arm is tied to his body to restrict movement and even though painful, his heart is happy.

Some children see him and run forward to greet him. His mirthful laughter mingles with the delighted giggles of the children. The children adore him. They love his round body, his puffy hands, curved lips and happy eyes. He is the only adult that romps around in the long grass with them and doesn't worry about the mundane things adults seem to worry about. He even accompanies them down to the river where they are not allowed to go unsupervised.

They beg him to tell them a story and hold their breath in anticipation. They want to see the merry sparkle in his eyes and hear the enticing wonder of his stories. Unbeknown to them he also teaches them about nature. How to take care of it, and that it doesn't belong to us alone, it belongs to everyone.

Bongwe smiles but shakes his head. As much as he would love to lose himself in the magical world of the young, now is not the time. Sweat pours down his face and he wipes it off with his good hand. He really has to do something about the extra weight.

Around him the rhythmic beating of drums echo up to the treetops. All around people sing and dance, shaking their leg rattles and clapping their hands. Dust and smoke hang in the air. It looks like everyone for miles around had converged on the village to join in the celebration.

Weaving through the celebrations he tries to get to Lindiwi's hut as fast as he can. His progress is stopped when Nomsa steps out in front of him. She grabs his injured arm with her thin, skeletal and dirty hand. He winches when a sharp pain shoots through him. What's the matter with the woman? Can't she see his arm is injured?

She doesn't, instead she squeals in a high voice. "Bongwe! Bongwe! Did you hear what happened?"

Bongwe rolls his eyes upwards. "Lindiwi obviously had a boy," he says irritated. She is blocking his way and he always disliked her toothless grin immensely.

"Yes! Yes! But that's not all!" she screams while bouncing up and down with excitement. It is not often that she has the opportunity to give such succulent news to someone as important as Bongwe! She leans closer and her foul breath floats through the air. "Lindiwi gave birth to twins, both boys!"

Bongwe steps back in shock. "What! Are you sure?" he asks.

"Of course I'm sure!" she squeals indignantly. "I was there you know!" Her grip on his arm intensifies and her beady eyes sparkle with delight. She is enjoying every moment!

He shakes her clutching hand off his injured arm. He needs to get away from the old hag and he feels the disgust rise in his stomach.

"Get away from me!" he growls and his small eyes flash in his round usually pleasant looking face. Not only does she find pleasure in someone else's misfortune, her conversational powers ignore time and embrace eternity. Without a further word he turns and walks away.

Nomsa is quite taken aback. Imagine speaking to her as if she is of no consequence! She gives her penetrating laugh and spits on the ground. Bongwe is just as miserable as Thukani. She sees some new arrivals enter the village and hurries forward to meet them. They probably don't know the full story!

At Lindiwi's hut Bongwe calls respectfully for permission to enter. His arm throbs painfully but he doesn't care.

On the inside Thukani hears his friend's voice and can hardly contain his excitement. He rushes to greet him, grabs him by the shoulders and pushes him in the direction of his newborn son. With a wide and rare smile he says proudly. "Come and look at my son Matsisi! He is a strong and healthy boy!" He hardly seems to notice or care about Bongwe's injured arm.

Bongwe looks at the little boy and congratulates his friend sincerely on the birth of his heir. He is acutely aware of Lindiwi sitting very still, half hidden in the darkness. He tries not to look at her but can feel an aura of sorrow around her. Her near presence creates such a powerful protective thought in him that it causes an equally powerful reaction. He turns to Thukani. "Where is the other child?" he asks in a tight voice. Immediately a cold and uncomfortable atmosphere spreads through the hut.

Thukani's smile disappears and is replaced by a deep frown. "There is no other child! There is only one and his name is Matsisi" he says in a cold voice. A challenge in his eyes forebodes any more conversation on the matter. His body is tense and he has a dark look on his face.

Bongwe ignores Thukani's tone. "Where's the other child Thukani! What did you do with him! Where is he?"

"Don't think just because you're my friend that I will excuse your insolent behaviour. Remember who you're talking to!" Thukani hisses.

Outside the crowd starts chanting, "Long live Matsisi, the son of Isilwane! Long live Matsisi!" With another piercing cold look Thukani spins on his heels and walks out the hut. Bongwe's following words are lost amidst the roar of the crowd.

Bongwe stares at the empty space in front of him. He hears Lindiwi move behind him and swings around. She is struggling to her feet and he rushes over to help her. "Lindiwi," he whispers hoarsely. Without intending to, he poured his heart and soul into this one little word. His eyes search her face, absorbing every expression, every line and every feeling. Anguish rips pieces of raw flesh from his heart when he sees how drained and exhausted she is.

Lindiwi looks at him with her big brown eyes. There are no tears left. They dried up with the coldness in her heart. "The people say I'm evil," she says without emotion.

With his free arm he pulls her into his embrace. "Of course, you're not evil," he says tenderly in her ear while holding her close.

Intense emotions suddenly rush headlong through his veins. How he longs to love her. How he longs to protect her. If only he could take away the dark shadows from her eyes. He closes his eyes. There is nothing he can do, nothing he can say. His love was doomed from the start.

Lindiwi pulls herself from his embrace and steps back. No! She won't allow herself to feel again. Yesterday she might have been able to be drawn to the love she sees in his eyes. Yesterday she still desperately longed, deep within her soul, to be loved like that. Today she is cold and broken. Today she doesn't care anymore. "Thukani took the second born of our sons and offered him to the crocodiles," she says bitterly.

Bongwe shakes his head in disbelief. He knows the customs of their people but his soul recoils at what Thukani has done. Surely they could have found another way? His head spins. What if he goes down to the river? Is there a possibility that he might still find the child alive and save him?

In the open doorway Smangaliso, Thukani's head warrior, clears his throat. His huge body fills the whole entrance. He bows his head respectfully and says in his low, slow voice. "Isilwane requires the presence of his wife and son." His face is expressionless and he gives no indication that he has heard or seen anything.

Lindiwi bends down and picks up her son. She doesn't make any effort regarding her appearance. With a cold heart and cold eyes she walks past Bongwe out of the hut.

In that same instant Bongwe makes up his mind. He will go to the river on the odd chance that the baby has survived. He will do whatever he can to save a helpless child. He doesn't feel the painful throbbing of his injured arm. His whole being is focused on what he must do. With a racing heart he walks outside and slowly starts weaving his way through the crowd towards the river.

In the shadows Smangaliso is watching Bongwe. With the instinct of a warrior he knows where Bongwe is going. He looks at the celebration. They are so busy filling their bellies with cornmeal beer and roasted meat they don't see the suppressed urgency in Bongwe's walk. Under the cover of darkness he allows, for only the tiniest of moments, his emotions to surface. Knowing right from wrong doesn't come from the mind, it comes from the heart. He will let Bongwe be.

Once Bongwe reaches the outskirts of the village he starts running towards the river. Once there he scans the area, but with only the moonlight to help him, it is not easy. Still it is enough to see the blood mingled with sand at the river's edge. He kicks at the loose sand as if he wants to cover the bloody traces screaming out at him. He is too late!

"A dog can have a litter of six pups but a woman can't have twins!" he screams in the direction of the village. "What's the matter with you people? Are you all mad?" Fierce anger builds up inside him. Not only anger for an innocent child but also anger for an unfulfilled love.

As the rage inside him erupts he looks up at the moon and screams wildly. "I curse you Thukani! I curse you! I curse you and Nomsa and all the idiots in this village! I curse you all to lie like rotten carcasses in the sun for the hyenas and vultures to eat! I curse you for killing an innocent child so that another may live! I curse you! I curse you!"

He falls to his knees and sobs rack his body. "I curse myself, Bongwe, to never find another woman because I dared to fall in love with my best friend's wife."

Much later he gets up and starts walking. He is hardly aware of anything around him, except the burning pain in his arm. Exhaustion combined with pain causes him to stumble between the bushes and trees. He trips over a tree root and falls down. Holding onto the tree he tries so get up but nausea overwhelms him. He doubles over and vomits. He wipes his mouth with the back of his hand. He feels lightheaded and the pain in his injured arm has increased to a steady pulsating tempo.

He staggers in the direction of Mthisa's cave while cursing himself that he didn't go there before he went to the village. He had long since lost track of time and is only vaguely aware that the sun has started setting making way for the moon. It is a long and slow journey.

Out of breath he eventually reaches her cave. By this time his injured arm is so painful that he can hardly focus on the entrance. Holding on the cave wall for support he calls her name in a hoarse voice. There is no answer and he calls again, but only silence greets him.

He waits at the entrance not sure what to do next. Not so far away a hyena, the dog like creature with a powerful jaw gives a hysterical laugh. It spurs him into action and he staggers inside while mumbling an apology to Mthisa with a burning throat.

He shouldn't have bothered. The cave is empty. All that remains of the fire, in the centre of the cave, is a small red coal. With trembling fingers he adds more wood and tries to coax it back to life. Slowly it begins to flicker and lights up the cave.

A bat swoops past him and he instinctively ducks. Not that the fruit bat with its long fox-like muzzle would possibly fly into him with its extreme manoeuvrability and navigation. Still he shivers. It is creepy the way bats hang upside down in caves, crevices and hollow trees.

Bongwe lies down while sweat runs in little rivers down his face. The lifelessness of the cave fills him. It feels barren and devoid of anything except its own emptiness. "Mthisa I need your help," he whispers before the darkness of sleep comes.

Drifting in and out of consciousness, time becomes meaningless. He is unaware of the strong wind howling outside bringing with it the stench of death. He exists only in a delirious blur and doesn't know or care that nothing in the world ever happens by chance.

The Spirit People gather around Bongwe feverish body. He is a brave man. Few people would dare to go to Mthisa's cave. Only those desperate to cure their illness would visit her, and then usually in secret. The Spirit People shake their heads. Earth People can be so strange sometimes. When they don't understand something, they fear it.

Mthisa was named after her mother, who was one of Nzunza's daughters. She was also the one who was sent to Manala to marry him according to the peace agreement. Soon after she gave birth to a daughter the peace agreement was broken and the village shunned her. She was moved to the outskirts of the village and merely tolerated. She was nothing to them.

The same fate befell the small innocent Mthisa. Other children were not allowed to play with her and she was not invited to partake in any activities. Her mother became a still, silent and bitter woman, doing her daily task and nothing more, nothing less. It didn't bother Mthisa. Left alone to do as she pleased, Mthisa was busy with other things. She was content to spend her time alone and it wasn't long before the Spirit People visited her and started teaching her.

People would see her talking to plants and animals and sometimes things they could not see. They became fearful of her herbal mixtures that could cure illness and young ones were warned to stay away from her and her treacherous family.

When her mother died she simply packed up and moved to a secluded cave. "Why should I try and fit into a menial social system that pretends to be valuable," she said to the Spirit People.

The Spirit People smile. "Oh, how they love the fierce little Mthisa!"

When Bongwe starts tossing and turning again they put their featherlike hands on his hot forehead. Mthisa will not return but help will be here soon.

The sun is shining bright and merry outside the cave when Bongwe eventually wakes up. His first instinct is to get up, but he stops very quickly when everything around him spins.

"Easy my brother," a soft voice says behind him.

"Mthisa?" he asks and the voice answers, "No, she's not here, she has left. I've been taking care of you."

Bongwe feels confused and his head begins to spin in all directions again. The stranger holds a calabash filled with cool, sweet liquid to his lips and he drinks thirstily. "Who are you?" he asks with a tongue that doesn't seem to want to form the words properly.

The stranger answers in a quiet, calm voice. "I am your brother."

"I don't have a brother," Bongwe mumbles. His body feels heavy and he can't keep his eyes open. The pull of nothingness is too strong and he stops resisting it. Soon he is sound asleep again.

The next day Bongwe wakes up again. He sits up and breathes a sigh of relief. His head has stopped spinning. He looks down at his arm tied against his body. It is not hurting anymore and he touches it gently. It seems to be fine. He looks up when there is a movement at the cave entrance and the stranger walks in. Bongwe's mouth gapes open and his small eyes widen. He has never seen anything like this before in his life!

The man is tall and thin. He has an olive complexion and his head is clean-shaven. He has clear, bright and mysterious hazel coloured eyes. Draped around his waist is an orange cloth that is long enough to cover his legs. His chest is bare except for one part of the robe that is hanging loosely over his left shoulder.

Bongwe stutters. "Who………Who are you?"

Without answering the stranger walks to the fire, scoops some cooked cornmeal into a bowl and hands it to Bongwe. When the delicious aroma drifts into Bongwe's nose he realizes how hungry he is and starts eating. He had only eaten a small portion when he feels full and puts the half eaten bowl down. He looks at the stranger and asks, "Who are you? How long have I been here? Where is Mthisa?"

The strange man slowly shakes his head and sits down cross-legged opposite him. "So many questions and so few answers. That is the way of life," he says in his soft voice.

Bongwe feels uncomfortable. He feels like the mysterious eyes of the stranger are digging deep within his soul to reveal the secret things he has buried there. He wipes his hand over his eyes as if he wants to block the entrance to his inner being. "Who are you?" he asks again.

The stranger answers in his calm voice. "Some call me Master." His hands, which were folded together in his lap, he now places palms upwards on his knees.

Master!" Bongwe exclaims. "Master of what, your slaves?"

Master shakes his head. "I have no slaves, only students."

"Oh." Bongwe says with relief. "What do you teach your students?"

Master's expression remains calm and soft. "To become Masters."

This confuses Bongwe even more and he shakes his head. He doesn't understand at all. "What is a master then?" he asks.

"A master is one who has gained the necessary understanding," he gets told.

"Of what!" Bongwe says exasperated.

Master lifts his eyebrows ever so slightly, "Of life" he says.

When Bongwe shakes his head, the strange man continues in his soft voice. "A Master is one who understands that everything that is, is alive. He is someone who knows that everything is connected and that there is no separation. He is one who always has the same message. Everything that is, is one. What I am, you are and what you are, I am. You are one with me, and I am one with you, because we are both one with everything that is. We are brothers."

"But we aren't even related!" Bongwe bursts out.

Master's lips twist in a small smile. "Relation has got nothing to do with it. We were all created by the Great Spirit therefore we are all brothers and sisters. Everything is equal and everything is the same, therefore it is all one. You see Bongwe, when you grasp the fact that everything that is, is one, you understand that nothing ever happens by chance. You understand that there is a reason for everything."

"A reason for everything!" Bongwe bust out. "There is no reason for killing a innocent baby! What they did is cruel and wrong!"

Master shakes his head gently. "There are no rights or wrongs with the Great Spirit. There are only intentions and life proceeds out of your intentions for it." He gets up and starts walking out of the cave.

"Wait!" Bongwe calls him back.

He turns around and looks at Bongwe. "A Master is also one who realizes that everyone is a Master." He bows his head at Bongwe and then he is gone. Outside the sun is setting and moon is already visible in the sky. It is once again that magical time when day and night meet.

With enough food and water left in the cave Bongwe waits another week before he feels strong enough to travel. He makes his way back to the village slowly and has to rest often to catch his breath. It frustrates him because he wants to get home as soon as he can.

As he gets closer to the village he seems to get that extra burst of energy and he quickens his pace. Suddenly he stops. Something is wrong! Everything is so quiet. He can't hear children play or the animated chatter of the busy women. Even the birds, which usually protect their eggs noisily, are quiet. Everything around him appears to be suffused with a still and deep silence.

With a feeling of doom he walks into the silent village and gasp at the brutal sight that greets him. All around him are ruins, ashes and dead rotting bodies. The stench churns in this stomach and the horror of it almost makes him want to stop breathing.

He falls to his knees with a groan and covers his face with his hands. Like a storm, soaking him to the bone, emotions flood over him. He tries to keep the door closed but it opens with a loud creak. Bongwe, the best and lifelong friend of Thukani, once again lifts his face up to the sky and screams. In that moment he begins to understand that life proceeds out of your intentions for it.

Chapter 5
Bring Forth the New by Breaking Down the Old

Mthisa tosses and turns, she is having another dream. She is dreaming about strange and unfamiliar people in a far off land. They don't look like the Ndebele people at all. Their skin is a white clay colour and it makes them appear sickly, yet they are all in good health. They talk in a strange language that makes no sense to her and she can't understand a word of what they are saying.

Two very large and identical huts stand side by side in one of the villages. None of the woman had bothered to paint and decorate the huts making them look grey and lifeless. The huts are bigger than anything Mthisa had ever seen in her life. They reach so high that they must surely be touching the sky. Could it be that their height was an effort to get closer to the Great Spirit?

Suddenly the sky makes a deep rumbling noise and a large rock, surrounded by fierce fire appears. It heads directly towards the two huts. With a shattering force and blinding flash it slams into the closest hut. The hut begins to shiver and shake and fire rapidly spreads in and around it. It screeches and groans for a while, then collapses in a swirl of dust.

Another rumbling noise from the sky produces another flaming rock. With equal force and same blinding light, it hits the remaining hut. The second hut crumbles to lie shivering beside its twin.

The people scream in terror and franticly search for a safe place to hide. Their fear gives them a ghostlike appearance.

Then it is silent. Where the twin huts once stood long and tall, there is now nothing. All that is left is the ruins of something that had once been. In the ashes of the crumbling huts there is a geometrical shape of a triangle.

Mthisa wakes up with a start. She looks over to the sleeping children just as the boy she rescued yawns and stretches. The light blanket covering him slips away to reveal his perfect little naked body. On his hip his triangular birthmark shines and sparkles in the ray of a single moonbeam.

Mthisa frowns. There must be some connection! Coincidences don't exist. A thought springs in her mind. A while ago the Spirit People told her that sometimes the best way to bring forth the new, is to break down the old.

She can understand that. It is like a fire. It can start with a small insignificant flame that can change into a blazing inferno. It will destroy everything in its path, whether it is man, animal, insects or her precious herbs. The wind conspires to help and the fire rides on its crest until it has destroyed everything it can find. You look at the black, scorched and desolated land and wonder why it is necessary. What is the purpose behind the destruction?

Yet after a week, small green shoots appear all over the darkened land. Birds return, seeking out the remains of their old nests. It is as if the land has suddenly sprung to life again with an eager willingness to continue. Animals step carefully over still smouldering old trees, and seek out the fresh and new green sprouts. Everywhere you look there is new life! The barren land has turned into a fertile place of perfection once more. The old were destroyed to make way for the new.

Her thoughts are broken when Zinhle sits up to attend to her daughter who has started crying. Soon both children are asleep again with full stomachs and sleepy eyes. Mthisa however, is still wide-awake. Sleep will not come easily now.

Before the sun even had a chance to peek over the horizon, she gets up. She reties the faded, but clean head cloth over her hair, and starts preparing breakfast. It is important that they cover as much distance as they can before the heat of the sun dehydrates them. They will do most of their walking in the early hours of the day and rest during the hottest part, when the children can be nursed. They will only stop when the sun disappears behind the horizon and they cannot navigate their way in the darkness anymore.

Soon they are on their way. They keep a sharp lookout for dangers that could lurk behind every bush. Steadfastly they walk, without talking, on a journey that is going to be long and gruelling.

To someone watching, it might appear as if they are simply walking, yet they are fulfilling a destiny. Unbeknown to them it is a destiny that both agreed to long, long ago, before they separated from the Great Spirit to become part of the earth people.

A couple of slender-tailed meerkats curiously watch their progress. The meerkats are resting after a busy morning. They have been hunting snakes and used their amazing agility to avoid its strike, even those whose poison they are not immune to!

If the walking women could just clear their minds for a moment and observe, they will realize that nature, which is always immersed in the universal current of the Great Spirit, is watching them. Nature hopes with an aching heart that the child Mthisa carries will be the one to teach humans they are one with them.

A springbuck leaps high into the air with excitement. Its back is arched, its legs straight and hooves bunched together. The fold of skin from the centre of his back to the rump opens like a pouch to reveal a crest of long, white, bristly hair.

Some day humans will learn that nature is a copious nursery containing all the wisdom of the world. Only then will the language of nature will be understood. Will it happen? They don't know, they can only hope.

After a long day of walking Mthisa and Zinhle make camp for the night. They are tired and hungry. To keep predators away they add more wood to the fire. Only once they have taken care of the two babies do they settle down to sleep.

Mthisa wakes up from her restless sleep with the sound of rhythmic drumming. She jumps up at the same time as the terrified Zinhle, who tightens her hold on her whimpering daughter.

The sound of approaching drums gets louder. One rhythmic drummer is joined by another, and another, until the beating of the drums is all that echo around them. When stamping feet and war cries mingle with the vibration of the drums on the earth's surface, Mthisa is spurred into action.

She puts her finger in front of her mouth to gesture to Zinhle to keep her daughter quiet. She implores her with her eyes, with her senses, and with everything she can, to be calm. It would be disastrous if the war party hears the sounds of a crying baby. In the stillness of the night sound carries far. Zinhle nods her head. Her eyes are large and her mouth strained but she understands.

No further time is wasted. With trembling fingers they tie the children to their backs. Leaving the still smouldering fire as it is, they run into the protection of the darkness. It doesn't even occur to them that the remains of the fire are an indication of their presence. All they can focus on is the noise of the war party that sounds as if it is snapping at their heels.

They run through the bushes and low hanging branches, which cut and bruise them. They feel like rats trying to avoid the deadly claws of a hawk overhead. The rhythmic drumming becomes their heartbeat and the stamping feet their breathing. Both infants' start crying.

Mthisa stops suddenly and Zinhle crashes into her. Directly in front of them is a pack of hyenas. What an easy prey they would be for the dog like creatures with its powerful jaws! In the moonlight they can see the hyena's brownish-grey colour and black spots, their large necks and heads and well-developed forelegs.

Chills run down their spines as the front hyena throws her head back and emits a striking howl which rises in pitch till it sounds like hysterical human laughter. Loudly the other hyenas join her. Again and again they howl, until their hysterical laughter completely swallows the desperate whimpers of the infants.

With dry mouths the women look at the hyenas open mouths, their hanging tongues dripping with saliva, and vicious looking teeth glowing in the moonlight. Mthisa thinks with a dull brain. If they move the hyenas will kill them! If they stay the army could capture them. She makes her decision. They will continue running. They hear the hyenas howl behind them but don't look back.

Bats swoop by and navigate their way around them and an owl hoots above them as they hurry past. Red eyes, reflected in the moonlight, follow their every move. Once more nature has immersed itself in the universal current of the Great Spirit and every part will play its role to ensure their survival.

The Spirit People start dancing in the moonlight. Their dancing creates shadows and flashing lights. Illusions that penetrate even the darkest corner. They dance between the stars, in the branches of the trees and in between the rocks and bushes. They dance as if their lives depend on it, with all their heart and with all their soul!

In the encampment Mzilikazi is nervous. His spies have already reported that Shaka is not far behind. Everyone's nerves are tense and strained and the sentry guards are restless.

One guard is sure he saw two women running but he is so frightened by the dancing shadows he hardly gives it a thought. His fear increases with the hysterical laughter of the hyenas and it multiplies the experience of what he sees, or thinks he sees. He stays at his post. He will share this with no one.

On top of a high ridge the women stop running. They sink down with numb legs and sore feet. It is daybreak and running and stumbling through the night has taken its final toll. Their breath rasps hoarse and dry in their throats and their chests ache painfully. They are exhausted and unable to continue. They have done all they can to protect the children. There is nothing more they can do.

Resigned to whatever fate awaits them they look down at the war party below them with expressionless eyes and exhausted faces. Like a colony of ants, they seem to be mingling about directionless. Sharp orders fill the air and in an orderly fashion the war party starts moving in the opposite direction. Away from the woman and children.

Some of the intense tension leaves their bodies but their breathing is still short and shallow. Unable to get up, they crawl, almost dragging their exhausted bodies, to the nearest tree. They only have enough energy left to untie the children and close their burning eyes. It is nothing short of a miracle they were not captured or killed.

Mthisa groans softly in a rasping voice. "I have never been so scared in my life." Like a soft whisper in the wind she hears the Spirit People ask tenderly. "Mthisa do you think you were alone?" A lump jumps to her throat and tears roll down her scratched cheeks. She sobs softly. "We are not alone................we never were."

Asleep, in the deep sleep only extreme exhaustion can bring, the wind flutters around the small group. Overhead the leaves rustle a soothing lullaby. The Spirit People cover them in a blanket made of fluffy white clouds. They are safe!

Behind them in the village they left behind Sibongile carries Matsisi with slow and lifeless steps. Her clothes are dirty and full of blood. She wants to shut out the screams of terror still ringing in her ears, but they won't stop. Without even being aware of it, she rocks Matsisi backwards and forwards. Her eyes look but don't see.

She jumps with fright when someone touches her shoulder. She swings around, and breathes a sigh of relief. It is her father, Thukani. His shoulders are sagged, like a very tired old man, and clotted blood clings to a gaping wound in his leg.

They stare at each other. What can they say? It all happened so quickly. One minute they were sleeping and the next minute they were running and fighting for their life. Her heart burns in her chest about the absence of meaning in the horrifying event.

Aware and interested in everything that goes on around her, the proud yet young Sibongile had heard the stories about Shaka, the mighty ruler of the Zulu People. As the first-born daughter of Thukani and his First Wife she often took advantage of her position and sneaked in to listen to serious discussions.

With some concern it was discussed how innovative Shaka was in tactics and weaponry. From travellers they heard how he had shaped his warriors into a formidable military force. They heard how he started to introduce women's regiments and how the number of his subjects quadrupled as he absorbed the conquered groups into the Zulu People. Yes indeed, Shaka was a man to be feared and not taken lightly!

One day they heard rumours that Mzilikazi, a general in Shaka's army, took his followers and left Shaka's forces secretly, under the cover of darkness. Smangaliso, the head warrior, suggested in his low, slow voice that they take some precautions to protect themselves. He explained that the angry Shaka will leave no stone unturned to find Mzilikazi and when he does so, he will show no mercy. Everyone despises a traitor!

Thukani agreed but ordered in his usual blunt and domineering way that it could wait until after Lindiwi had given birth. His heir was all he could focus on. Nothing was more important.

Smangaliso bowed his clean-shaven head in acceptance. The ignored young girl Sibongile, tucked away in a corner, watched with interest and noticed that even though the head warrior's face remained expressionless he was clenching his heavy jaw. She so wished she knew what the big man was thinking. Maybe it was a blessing that she did not.

With the instinct of a true warrior Smangaliso knew that warring armies of Shaka and Mzilikazi were on the move. Rumours of empty villages and murdered children are something to be taken seriously. In his heart he knows the Ndebele People are no match for Shaka or Mzilikazi. All that will be left is death and ashes. He looks up and his eyes catch those of the young girl. He is not afraid to die, he has never been. It is the life of a warrior.

A shout from Bongwe breaks Sibongile and Thukani's trance like stare. Frightened and injured people slowly begin to crawl out of undiscovered hiding places. Matsisi starts crying louder. He is hungry!

Chapter 6
You cannot Change the Essence of Who you are

Mthisa looks at the sullen young man staring into the fire opposite her. The bowl of food in his hands is untouched. In fact he seems unaware that he is holding it at all. He is tall and well built, just like his father Thukani, without the slightly hooked nose. His hair is long and reaches halfway down his back. It is fairly straight like those of his mother Lindiwi. Strange as it may seem, he has the same intense look in his brown eyes as Mthisa.

Mthisa shakes her head. It all seems so long ago. Another time, another village. She had adapted to not being alone but sometimes she still longs for it with all her heart. Irritated she admonishes him. "Mandla! Eat your food it's getting cold." When he doesn't respond she calls again, more sharply this time. "Mandla!"

He jerks his head up with a stubborn frown. "Stop telling me what to do!" he grinds through clenched teeth.

"What's wrong?" Mthisa asks as evenly as she can, while suppressing her own short temper. Her eagle sharp eyes search his face.

"Nothing's wrong!" Mandla growls and tosses the bowl of cornmeal in the fire as hard as he can. Sparks fly in all directions and the fire splatters and crackles.

Frustrated Mthisa rolls her eyes upwards. She knows that arguing with him usually just makes matters worse, but the sharp snap leaves her mouth anyway. "Well it's obvious something is bothering you!"

He jumps up with flashing eyes. "Nothing's bothering me! Just leave me alone!" he snarls and storms out of the hut.

Mthisa gives a deep sigh and wipes her hand over her eyes. Sometimes Mandla can really be a raving irritation! Everyday new scenarios seem to be developing. His temper is short and he is restless. It's as if ordinary day-to-day living is frustrating him. She knows the feeling well and understands more than what he realises. Did the same things not happen to her? She starts cleaning up the mess. She can only help him if he allows her to.

Mandla heads out of the village. He walks fast, his body tense and tight. His usual observant eyes are clouded in thought, and see nothing.

He doesn't notice or care that some young girls look at him with desire in their eyes. Hands that were painting a moment ago stop, as they watch his graceful but manly walk. Disappointed they start painting again before their mothers notice their idle hands.

Mandla is not really walking in any direction at all. He is simply stomping through the bushes to get away. He wants to be alone. He needs to think. He rips some leaves off a thin tree branch. With a grunt he tosses the leaves on the ground and sits down on a large rock. He lowers his head between his hands. The restless feeling is becoming stronger and stronger everyday. He has tried resisting it but is so intense that it continues to haunt him. "What is wrong with me?" he mumbles under his breath.

He looks up when he hears a snort. Close by some zebras are grazing. They are pale yellow, with broad, black stripes right down to their hooves. Some of the broad stripes are interspersed with fainter markings. It is unusual that they didn't scatter and run with his arrival.

His frown disappears and it gives his face a softer look. In this exact moment his problems and frustrations slip into the background and he immerses himself in the beauty of nature. For now, he is content to breathe deeply of the fresh air and watch the zebras.

He jumps with fright when a lioness charges the zebras from behind him! She passes so close that he can feel her wind of swiftness. As fast as he can, he runs to the nearest tree and starts climbing it with sweaty hands. It leaves him ice cold that he was unaware of her presence until now!

Another two lionesses, which were waiting in the bushes for her signal, now join the leader huntress. They are targeting a small zebra foal. Alone the foal's chance of survival is slim!

The zebras don't waste time. The whole group starts running. While running they push all the young foals into the centre protecting them. They move together, but change direction often as if some invisible hand is directing them. Their stripes blend and mingle causing a kaleidoscope of stripy images.

The lionesses shake their heads and pant with the effort of penetrating the flashing stripes that act as the zebra's protective coloration. The stripes confuse and disorientate them! After a while they give up. Their tongues drip wet drops of saliva in the dry dust. They growl and move away. They will try again later.

Mandla breathes a sigh of relief. He makes sure the lionesses have definitely left before he gets out of the tree. It's a wonder that the grumbling stomachs of their cubs didn't make him their prey!

Suddenly, like a flash in his head, Mandla knows what he needs to do. Understanding has come at last. He is as confused as the lionesses. He needs to talk to Mthisa! He didn't want to talk to her before. He simply felt, as young people often do, that she wouldn't understand. He ignores his own stubborn streak but acknowledges with a pang of regret, that he has been making life difficult for her. He knows her sharp penetrating eyes, which sometimes feels as if it looks right into your deepest being, has seen something is wrong. Without wasting anymore time he returns to their hut.

Mthisa is busy preparing some herbal remedies. She glances up when he enters but continues working.

Mandla walks over to the fire and sits down, only to get up again. He walks over to Mthisa, takes her by the shoulders and turns her around. His eyes are apologetic. "I'm sorry."

"Do you want to talk about it?" Mthisa asks evenly.

Mandla nods his head and they both sit down. He clears his throat a bit unsure of how to begin. His mind feels like a whirlpool and he clears his throat again to try and get some kind of logical order. It doesn't happen and he simply blurts out. "Nodathile wants us to get married."

Mthisa feels her heart jerk at his unexpected announcement. It's not what she expected! She immediately lowers her eyes. Eyes sometimes show more than what one would like.

Even though everything inside her screams that it will be the biggest mistake of his life, she formulates an answer very carefully. Young people can be very strange sometimes. They ask for advice and when you give it, they do exactly the opposite. She looks up. "Well Mandla, you have known her for quite a while now and I remember when you met her, you told me that Nodathile is the woman of your dreams. She is beautiful and strong. She comes from a good family and you certainly have enough to pay her father handsomely."

He nods his head but his eyes have clouded over with frustration. "Yes she is beautiful, and I care about her.................but it's just........................she wants me to change the way I make my living," he says with some reluctance.

"Exactly what do you mean by that?" Mthisa snaps and immediately regrets it. She needs to stay calm. Fiercely she wishes she could tell Mandla that the outstandingly pretty Nodathile is cold and selfish!

Mandla ignores her snap. He is used to Mthisa. He starts rubbing his right eye to clear his thoughts. The best way to deal with things now is honesty. "Nodathile wants me to stop treating sick people with herbs and become a cattle farmer. She says she won't have sick people calling at her door day and night when they have no one but themselves to blame for their illnesses."

"Are you considering this option then?" Mthisa asks in a guarded voice, controlling her flashing emotions.

"Yes." Mandla says.

Mthisa tries to stay calm. "You can take a duckling away from its mother, living at the water's edge, the day it is born and keep it in a cage till it is fully grown. During this time it will never know water or learn how to swim. Then one day you take the duck to the water and what does it do? It doesn't hesitate at all. It simply gets into the water and swims."

"What has that got to do with me?" Mandla asks in a puzzled tone.

"Just as a duck cannot change the essence of who he is, you cannot change the essence of who you are either," she answers. "You could try and change and maybe even fool yourself that you are happy, but it will only be temporary. One unexpected day your own true self will begin a struggle to find a light in the darkness."

Mandla lifts his eyebrows. "I don't think she wants to change me. I think she just wants me to do something that is more profitable."

Mthisa jumps up and her eyes flash darkly. "Do what you like!" she fumes and starts pacing directionless in short, quick steps. "If you want to marry her, marry her! Just don't come crying to me when you realize that she has manipulated you straight into the burning fires of the sun! She will pick your bones as clean as the vultures devouring a rotting carcass! She is no different than her grandmother Nomsa, the old hag!"

"I didn't know you knew Nodathile's grandmother," Mandla says somewhat surprised.

Mthisa grunts. She increases her pace and tugs at her clothes. Sometimes the world can be such a bewildering place to live in and now she has said too much, or did she say too little. She stops and comes to a sudden decision. She walks back to the fire and sits down. The time is ripe for the truth. It is like waiting for a fruit to ripen for what seems an eternity, and then suddenly one morning it is ripe and juicy. Yesterday was too soon and tomorrow too late. The time is right now!

"Mthisa? What is going on?" Mandla asks confused.

"Nodathile's grandmother Nomsa and I stayed in the same village," she says calmly while staring into the fire.

"Oh. What village?" Mandla asks baffled.

She slowly looks up. "The village where your father and mother lived and where you were born."

Mandla feels as if someone has just ripped the breath from his lungs. An ice-cold shiver runs across his spine and his stomach contracts. He looks at her with a blank face and his mouth hangs open. He is so stunned that even though he tries to speak, no words come out. "I thought you were my mother!" he eventually blurts out.

"I am not," Mthisa says evenly.

Mandla jumps up. Suddenly he is furious. His eyes flash like lightning looking for something to strike. For a moment he fights to gain control but the battle is lost before it even began. "I hope the hot sun burns the skin off your body!" he shouts at her. "My whole life has been a lie! When did you intend telling me?"

"I will tell you now." Mthisa says softly and gestures to him to sit down. She wishes with all her heart she could take away his pain and confusion.

Mandla sits down, stands up and sits down again. It is as if his body won't keep still. Everything that he had always believed is shattered. He wants to storm out of the hut, yet a part of him desperately wants to know the truth. He stares at Mthisa and notices for the first time that her face is lined with tiny wrinkles, announcing the unstoppable footsteps of time. He shakes his head. Why did she keep the truth from him for all these years?

For a while Mthisa doesn't talk. She looks into the fire. She takes her thoughts backwards, as far as she can. It all happened so long, long ago. When she begins to talk she opens a floodgate of truth that will change Mandla's life forever. "Your father's name is Thukani and your mother's Lindiwi................"

Outside the hut the sun has disappeared and the shadows are lengthening as darkness silently creeps in.

Beside the open doorway Zinhle is like a statue. She is immovable, like an age-old tree with roots extending deep into the earth. It is wasn't her intention to intrude, on what is obviously an intimate conversation, but she has been unable to tear herself away from Mthisa's riveting story. The only thing Mthisa had ever told her about Mandla was that he was a special child she had to care for. She never questioned it, she trusted Mthisa with her life. Now she hears, for the first time, the unbelievable events leading to the long journey they undertook with the infants

Gently, ever so gently, she is joined by the Spirit People. They tenderly cradle her in their arms when she sinks down and sobs. She can't believe she is the beautiful soul Mthisa talks about.

The Spirit People stroke her hair with feather light fingers. They never saw the large flat nose or uneven teeth. They always thought she was beautiful! Their eyes soften when they feel her gratitude, deep within her soul, that the Great Spirit considered her worthy enough to fulfil such an important task.

When Mandla walks past her into the darkness she struggles to her feet. With tears still wet on her face she enters the hut. The women's eyes lock.

Mthisa gives a sigh of relief. She is free at last of the secret burden she had to carry. It is good that Zinhle knows. After all, she fulfilled a most important part.

She gestures to Zinhle to sit down and shoves a calabash filled with cornmeal beer into her hand. Zinhle drinks deeply, wipes her mouth with the back of her hand and gives it back to Mthisa, who drinks deeply as well. The two old friends say nothing. There is nothing more to say.

Under a carpet of stars Mandla just walks. Earlier today when he stormed out of the hut he was going in no particular direction, he just wanted to get away. It is the same now, and without realizing it, he ends up at the exact same place.

He sits down on a rock and puts his head in his hands. Questions swirl in his head but more than that resentment, anger, and flashes of hatred for the way his life was weighed and found so light. Everything that he thought earlier today was complicated, looks almost ridiculously easy to the way it is now.

Mthisa saved his life, yet he has little understanding of the reason. All he feels at the moment is a raw pain in his heart for something that could have been, but is not. He thinks about his faceless mother and his father. Do they miss him? Did they even care?

What about his twin brother? What is his name? Does he know he has a brother? Mandla shakes his head. He can think about it as much as he likes, but no answer will come forward. He leans back against the tree behind him. He looks up and a bright star shoots across the sky leaving a trail of luminous glow behind it.

He gets up and starts walking back to the hut. He has made his decision. He will never find peace unless he finds his family first. Will they accept him? Right now he doesn't know or care, it is just something he has to do. Mthisa always says you can buy anything but human understanding. How true is that!

The Spirit People smile and dash between the trees following Mandla home. They will make sure nothing happens to him on the long journey ahead. They jump from moonbeam to moonbeam and whisper to him in the rustle of the leaves that everything will be fine.

While the Spirit People dance and swirl among the stars, the ever watching, Sibongile wonders if the star she saw shooting across the sky had any meaning. Soon she will know!

Chapter 7
The Meaning of Life

Mandla stretches and gives a lazy yawn. He has been traveling a couple of days and already the hot and dry weather has taken its toll on his energy. Nearby is a river and he heads toward the clear flowing water. He dives in and the cool water is like a breath of fresh air on his body and mind.

He gets out of the water very quickly when he sees a crocodile on the opposite bank. The last thing he wants is to be is a crocodile's tasty meal! His mouth pulls in an angry tight line and his thoughts turn bitter and dark. He seems to have a history with crocodiles!

Without drying himself he ties a soft deerskin around his waist and collects his things. He starts walking again while the wet drops still glint and sparkle on his tall and well built muscular body. He tries to concentrate on his surrounding, but his thoughts settle uncomfortably on Nodathile. She nearly went crazy when he told her he was leaving.

"Don't expect me to wait for you!" she screamed and looked at him so darkly that it shocked him. "There are lots of rich men that would pay handsomely just for the pleasure of having me. What makes you think I'll waste my time waiting for you! I don't think so!"

How well he remembers the way she clenched her teeth and how her inviting mouth pulled into an ugly tight line when she hissed. "Forget it Mandla. Just go, I can get along fine without you. I don't need you! I need a man that will satisfy my needs, not a daydreamer gathering herbs and searching for..................well, whatever you are searching for. Just go, you're wasting my time! I have better things to do!" She shrugged her shoulders as she walked away coldly. She didn't care that her words deeply cut his soul!

He shakes his head trying to get rid of the oppressive feeling that comes when he thinks about Nodathile. Only now he understands Mthisa's reaction. She already knew how superficial Nodathile's love was, and that she would have made Mandla's life a living nightmare with her selfish demands.

He grins, even though Mthisa said that he sometimes has an arrogant attitude, she has always been lavish with her love and wanted him to be happy. Of course she was not in the least surprised when he told her he was going in search of his family. She did point out that there is no guarantee that his family will still be alive after the marching armies of Mzilikazi and Shaka, but it makes no difference. Something deep inside him, like a silent invisible force, is compelling him forward.

Mandla pulls his shoulders back and starts walking faster. He grumbles under his breath, "I need to stop wasting time on useless thoughts because it is slowing me down."

Days come and go as Mandla walks along steadily. He notices nothing around him and the process of walking becomes an automated action, nothing more. However the energy of his thoughts is in constant motion.

He wonders why he was born and what the purpose of his life is. At times he becomes angry and bitter. Other times he dwells in the past. He fights it and resents it, but most of all he experiences the pain of it. He knows now, that remembering is painful, but that forgetting is even more painful. During times like these he walks with even more purpose. It is all he can do before his mind kills the idea of finding his family.

When it is too dark to walk anymore he makes a fire and lies his weary body down on some soft grass. He worries about how long his journey will take, but soon his breathing becomes slow and gentle, and the questions still and silent. However Mthisa's parting words always echo in his mind. "The only thing that could make your quest impossible to achieve, is the fear of failure."

And while the soft moon's rays envelop him like a silvery spider's web, the Spirit People giggle in the trees above him and it sounds like a thousand tinkering bells. They don't care about time. Time is the enemy of eternity and understands it not. You need to let go of the concept of time before time releases you.

The universe also responds to Mandla's thoughts. It does so because it always conspires to help the one who is searching for the truth of life. Soon the smooth and effortless flow of one day into another is going to suddenly stop, and the illusion of time will disappear for what could just be a heartbeat!

Mandla is staring into the fire. His stomach growls and he wishes he had some meat to eat. Hunting had been unsuccessful the last couple of days, and he had to fill his stomach with a spinach like plant called marogh, growing near the edge of the river. It just doesn't seem to fill him up. The soft deerskin around his waist is starting to look tattered and torn. He rubs his hands over his eyes to try and clear his pounding head. The energy of his intense thoughts had drained him. There are too many questions and no answers.

A lion roars in the distance and he turns his head to listen. It seems to be far away but he chucks some more wood on the fire anyway. It is already dusk, the time when day and night meet. Although the sun is still setting, the moon is already visible in the sky. Uncomfortably he remembers Mthisa telling him that when the sun and moon combine their powers, strange things can happen.

He jumps up when the lion roars again. It is much closer this time! He spins around when a second lion roars behind him and becomes ice cold when he hears a third answer. He scans the area but can't see anything. The roars of all three lions now echo all around him. It is loud and intense and hurts his ears. The earth shivers and shakes beneath his feet with a deep, low vibration.

He throws the last of the wood he collected on the fire, hoping it will deter the lions from coming closer. According to the hunters, lions dislike fires. They also claim that lions do not usually roar before a hunt, but it does little to reassure him. Each roar announces that the lions are moving closer. He stands as close to the fire as he can. Even though the age old instinct of survival has taken over there is nothing more he can do but wait and experience the unknown, whatever it may be.

Mandla swears under his breath when his triangular birthmark starts burning fiercely. He jerks his clothes away. It feels like it is on fire! His eyes widen, the birthmark is glowing bright and luminous like a firefly. He rubs it hard. What on earth is going on? What is happening? He jerks around when he hears a noise in the bushes. He swallows hard when he sees the lion. He doesn't move, his body feels frozen.

The lion doesn't take his yellow eyes, glowing in the now almost darkness, off Mandla. He lifts his nose into the air and takes in Mandla's scent. He swings his tail from side to side and it makes a swishing noise. He is a large and majestic male with a long muscular body and large head. His black mane, which covers his head and neck, extends to his shoulders and belly. He shakes his head and his mane sways gently from side to side.

Mandla's throat becomes even dryer and his breathing shallow and uneven when two more lions appear, one to the left of him and the other to the right. Surrounded by three huge males, the king of all beasts looks at him with yellow glowing and hypnotic eyes. His thoughts scatter in all directions. Maybe he has invaded their territory or, it could be three nomadic bachelors looking for an easy meal. For a brief moment he considers running but the thought leaves his mind as quickly as it came. Only a fool gives a lion a moving target!

His birthmark starts to burn violently again. It is as if someone is pushing a red-hot knife into it. He doesn't want to move yet the stinging and burning sensation is almost too much to bear. At the same time he feels a strange pulling sensation in the centre of his forehead and it confuses him even more.

Then it all stops. The birthmark stops burning and the pulling sensation in the centre of his forehead stops. Everything around him has become deathly silent. There isn't even a whisper of a wind and the lions stand so still it looks like they are cast in stone. It is as if all movement has stopped in a great silent warp of time. The only sound is Mandla's rugged and uneven breathing.

He looks up when there is a bright flash in the sky. The moon shivers and shakes and to Mandla it looks like it is alive, like a living breathing being. Another bright flash and three silvery moonbeams creep out of the moon detaching themselves from their mother's womb. Lazily they stretch themselves across the sky. They continue to stretch and brighten, each enjoying their own freedom. Once more the sky brightens in a flash and without hesitation the three moonbeams move closer and connect. They combine their own identities and become a triangle of silver, bright, and luminous moonlight.

The triangle of moonlight slowly drifts down to earth and settle around Mandla interconnecting the three lions. He is enclosed in a triangle of moonlight with a lion on each corner. The lions begin to shine with the same silvery glow.

Mandla touches his forehead. He can feel the pulling sensation again and it is even more intense than before. He jerks with fright when he hears a clear, calm voice say, "Everything that is, is alive. Everything that is alive can communicate."

He looks around but there is no one there! The unknown has caused his nerves to be tense and strained. Nothing that is happening now makes sense to the normal, logical and reasoning function of his brain. He stares at the lion in front of him. The voice seems to be coming from there. Maybe he is simply going mad!

The clear voice speaks again. "Everything that is, is alive. Everything that is alive can communicate."

For the fourth time there is a blinding bright flash. This time it is so bright that Mandla shields his eyes. It takes a while for his eyes to adjust to the soft moonlight again and when it does so, there is a misty cloud floating towards him. Inside there is a barely discernable image of a man.

The whole area around Mandla feels as if it has become energized but he hardly gives it attention. Everything is focused on the floating mist coming closer. "Who................... Who are you?" Mandla manages to stutter.

"You can call me Tanua," he hears the clear voice say.

Mandla tries to clear the constricting tightness in this throat but only manages a hoarse croak. "What are you?"

Tanua answers in his deep, distinct and clear voice. "I am as you are, as we all are."

Mandla shakes his head in disbelief. It can't be! They are not the same! "What do you want from me?" he croaks again.

"We want nothing from you, we require nothing from you, and we need nothing from you," is his answer.

"We!" Mandla almost shouts glancing around uncomfortably. "Why do you say we? Are there more of you!"

Tanua's voice echoes no concern nor offers any comfort. "I speak of we' because I am not alone. Everything that is, is made up of parts. One cannot function without the other. We are everything around you. We are everything that is."

Mandla takes a deep breath hoping it will calm his shattered nerves. He's not comfortable about what's happening but at least it seems that neither the strange image, called Tanua, nor the lions mean him any harm.

Tanua speaks again. "I am here to bring you a gift. It is a very precious and valuable and comes from the Great Spirit himself."

Mandla's eyes widen in surprise at the unexpected words. "A gift! Why would the Great Spirit give me a gift?"

"Because He cares about you Beloved!" Tanua says and his voice softens a bit.

"Beloved?" Mandla repeats. "Why do you call me Beloved?"

"Are you surprised Mandla?" Tanua says and the mist around him shimmers. "Surely you know that the Great Spirit intimately knows and loves each and every one of His creations?"

Mandla shakes his head. He doesn't know what to say.

Tanua continues. "The gift the Great Spirit is offering you is the gift of courage. It is not the courage that makes you a brave and fearful warrior. No, it is the courage that will allow you to discover who and what you really are."

"I know who I am." Mandla says with a bit of arrogance.

Tanua ignores his tone and continues. "Don't confuse who you are with your identity Mandla. You think if you find your identify you will know who you are, but you will be disappointed, for an identify does not make a man.

You will have to look deeper for the answer and the courage that is being offered to you now, will allow you to do that. It will allow you to discover your own true self. Very few people in the world possess this kind of courage. They don't have the courage to look deep within their souls to see who and what they really are.

Your life can be likened to a plant. Every cycle it produces seeds. Yet, if someone takes all the seeds away, it will wither and die. There will be nothing left of the plant because it could not reproduce. It was the intension of the plant to be all that it could be, but because it wasn't allowed to give its seed life, it couldn't achieve it. Living in a complacent world where you don't discover the truth of life is like a plant without seeds.

You will only realize the truth of this once you embrace the courage the Great Spirit is offering you and draw it inward. To do this, awaken in your mind the possibility that you are more than what you appear to be. Some things cannot be seen, only felt. Who you are is what you are feeling, and what you are is how you express those feelings.

Allow all those places in your mind that were afraid to discover who and what you are to surrender. Search with the courage that you feel in your heart for the truth and you will find it. You will never find the meaning of life till you find yourself. It is the only water that will ever quench your thirst.

Will you accept this gift of courage from the Great Sprit Mandla? Are you brave enough to discover the truth of what is apparent and what is not?"

Mandla swallows hard to try and ease his dry throat. Each and every word Tanua had said engraved itself in his spinning head. All he is capable of doing at this exact moment is nod his head.

At his acceptance the three lions roar simultaneously. The ground shivers and shakes beneath Mandla's feet at the mighty sound. The whole area light up with a bright flash and once more he has to shield his eyes from the strong glare.

Then it is all gone. Everything has returned to normal. Night birds sing their lone songs and crickets chirp with the sound of the listless wind.

Slowly Mandla sags down in front of the still blazing fire. He puts his hand on his chest where he can feel the throbbing, loud, yet rhythmic pulse of his heart. It feels like it wants to jump out of his chest.

While the moon continues to create night as it has done since the beginning of time, Mandla is discovering that every journey has a way of creating its own momentum.

Chapter 8
No One Needs a Candle till Darkness Falls

The seasonal cycle completes its unstoppable movement as Mandla continues his long journey. He has lost a lot of weight. The long walk, and sometimes-hungry nights, has taken its toll. His long hair looks a bit messy and dishevelled and his body dirty and sweaty. With barely enough water to drink, washing is the least of his concerns. Sometimes he would be lucky and catch a rabbit and other times his knowledge of plants helped filled an empty stomach.

He scans the area with sunken eyes. The surrounding countryside is scattered with rocks and round bushes with thin, dry leaves. On the horizon he can see a solitary dry tree. There it stands alone, like a finger pointing to the Great Spirit asking why He has forgotten this barren and empty place.

As Mthisa found the confinement of her own company a blessing, he finds it a curse. He learns that one cannot order one's mind as one pleases, and his thoughts dig deeper and deeper into his innermost being. It swirls around like a maelstrom asking him what he wants to do with the rest of his life. It menacingly chills him with what he has already achieved, if anything. It torments him relentlessly about what he knows and believes about the Great Spirit.

During these times he would look at the sky and shout. "Why do you want me to know who and what I am? I am just Mandla! Leave me alone!"

He would long to talk to Mthisa and the wind would rustle in the grass and taunt him. "You cannot base your life on someone else's experience, only your own."

"Maybe the Great Spirit is expecting me to do something that I can't!" he would shout back and there would be no answer. Then it would feel as if it will still drive him mad and that the journey he started on very courageously had become a nightmare.

One evening, without really caring whether it is important or not, Mandla managed to bring a small fire to life. Tired and hungry he stares at the fire. He thinks of nothing, he simply looks at small licking flames. He feels a bit lightheaded but pays no attention to it. Hunger does that sometimes.

He starts feeling a slow pulling sensation in the centre of his forehead and all around him it becomes cloudy and hazy. He doesn't move. It is like his body is devoid of any energy. Surprised he realizes that he cannot even feel his body, almost as if it isn't there. All that he is with at the moment is his mind!

The misty cloud in front of him clears and he sees two frightened women, each with an infant tied to their back, running through the bushes. It is night-time and they stumble and fall. His heart races as he watches them. He feels the women's panting breath, and he feels the pain of every cut and bruise they receive. Even the fear pumping through their hearts becomes his fear. Unaware of the small groan he utters he recognizes a younger Mthisa and Zinhle. He is having his first vision!

The hazy mist encloses him again and when it clears there is another scene playing out in front of him. Again he feels the strong emotion of fear. However this time it is the fear of the infant Mthisa is carrying. His own fear as an infant is as real as it is now! Unbelievable!

He sees Mthisa untying him from her back and cradling him in her arms. She speaks in a soft loving voice and whispers to him that everything is fine and that he is safe. She comforts him and fills him with her strength. She pours out, from deep within her, all the love she has.

He feels her love filling him till it overflows and saturates his whole being. He feels like crying when his child-self returns her love without expectation or condition. It is simply a gift of love that is received and returned.

His body gives an unexpected jerk and pulls him away from the vision back to reality. He looks wide-eyed at the fire but immediately closes his eyes again and concentrates. He desperately wants to recapture the wonderful loving feeling between him and Mthisa. He craves for it like a drug, of which he cannot get enough.

Eventually he gives up, no matter how hard he tries he cannot get the vision back. Frustrated he lies down on the half-hearted bed he prepared earlier. He closes his eyes and as he does so understanding comes at last. Fear is stopping him from knowing himself and ultimately the love of the Great Spirit.

He gives a deep sigh. "Tomorrow," he whispers, "I'll try again tomorrow.........."

The Spirit People smile and jump off the bright moonbeams. They close around Mandla and make sure the guardians are watching. They touch him with their feather light fingers and croons. "Sometimes courage is the small voice inside which says I'll try again tomorrow."

Day will always gives way to night, and night will leave, so day can be created. It will flow into each other as it has done since the beginning of time. However this time Mandla will know that it is feelings not words that are the language of the soul.

While the moonbeams glitter and shine around Mandla the sun is preparing a spectacular sunrise. It is going to decorate the horizon with bright red, orange and pink.

The Spirit People chatter away. Mandla doesn't have far to go. Things are going well!

At long last Mandla leaves the barren and empty countryside behind. Everything changes to lush green and the age-old treetops sway back and forth as the playful wind frolics there. Food is abundant and the bones sticking out of Mandla's undernourished ribcage disappears. He gains the weight he lost and the hungry pains don't keep him awake at night. The muscles in his broad shoulders are strong again and his eyes clear and alert.

Content with a full stomach Mandla relaxes in front of the crackling fire. The sun is setting and a cool night wind has started blowing. He had walked quite far today trying to make up for lost time. He yawns, gets up and lies down on some soft, dry leaves under a marula tree. Sleep would be most welcome now.

An owl screeches above him. He gives an irritated frown and grunts. "I hope you're not going to keep me awake the whole night."

With an eerie "Shreeee" the owl responds, stretches its wings and noiselessly flies into the air. It circles the area but then glides down again and settle on the dry wood Mandla had collected. The owl is golden and white with a heart-shaped facial disk and small black eyes surrounded by stiff feathers. He has a hooked beak and sharp talons. Another eerie "Shreee" fills the air.

Mandla is tired and wants to sleep. He picks up a rock and throws it at the owl. He misses and the owl turns his entire head to look sideways to where the rock landed. It screeches again but stays where it is. The screeching of another two owls begins to fill the air behind Mandla. At the same time a red-hot fire sears through his birthmark. He jumps up "Oh no! Not now!" he groans.

Above him the moon flashes and shivers. It gives birth once more to three sparkling moonbeams that drift down to earth and settle around him. All three owls, at each end of the moonbeam triangle now look like they are cast in stone. Once again all movement has stopped in the silent warp of time. Mandla gives a deep sigh and stands up. Some things come to pass whether one wants it to or not.

"Everything that is, is alive, " he hears Tanua say. At the same time a misty cloud forms and Tanua's image floats towards him. Expecting to see only the faint outline of a man as before, he is quite surprised by the now clearer image Tanua presents to him. In fact all he can do is gape at Tanua with an open mouth.

Tanua has longish clay white hair with bright red stripes that looks like it is painted on by hand. He has an olive complexion and on his face is a neat, short brown beard. His face appears expressionless except for his green eyes, which seem vividly alive. They sparkle and flash in the moonlight.

Mandla has never seen anything like this before in his life. Mthisa told him that there are some strange beings in the Spirit World but this takes his breath away.

Tanua ignores Mandla reaction. He says in his clear, deep and distinct voice. "The Great Spirit wants you to stop calling Him Great Spirit. He wants you to call him God instead."

"God? Why? What does God mean?" Mandla asks confused and somewhat surprised.

Tanua answers, "God says that you think that spirits are left over parts of the dead and He is not dead. When you therefore refer to Him as God, there will be no association with anything that is dead but rather with everything that is alive. Think not of God as a word. It is a vibration. When you speak the word 'God,' you establish the highest possible vibration through your own body that connects you directly to Him. God is the highest principle flowing through you. The Great Spirit is always referred to, by those who know, as God."

Mandla repeats the word "God" to himself. As he does so a strange tingling sensation runs up and down his spine. Amazed he shakes his head at the effect.

Tanua talks again. "Everything that is, is alive. No one needs a candle until darkness falls."

Mandla lifts his eyebrows. "What's that supposed to mean?" he asks.

"It means that you have spent a long time reflecting and have not discovered the truth. You are like one groping in the darkness. I am bringing you the light you need so that you can move out of the darkness and into the light. To know who you really are, you must also know who you are not.

To discover this you will need patience and it is the gift God is giving you now. Patience is the only thing that will bring results in your search for self. Nothing can ever invade the peace that patience brings. Patience doesn't look to the physical world for answers but to God, where all questions are asked and all prayers are heard.

Sometimes life may even call upon you to prove who you are by letting you demonstrate an aspect of who you are not. Therefore you cannot know yourself as who you are, until you have come to know who you are not. It is by that which are you not that you define yourself.

Only patience can open the door for you to see and understand. It will show you that your life is a statement of who you are. Will you accept this gift Beloved?"

Mandla nods his head. As before the words seems to be etching itself in his head forever. He has to shade his eyes as the whole area explodes with brilliant light. The three owls screech loudly at the same time.

Then it is still, everything the same as it was. Hungry flames lick noisily at the dry wood and a cool wind moves the trees.

Mandla lies down again and closes his tired eyes. The body wants to rest but the mind doesn't give up so quickly. Sleep won't come easy tonight!

The Spirit People keep watch over the restless Mandla. They guard him as they have done every night, since the day he was born. They stroke his long hair as he tosses and turns. They will do whatever they can to help him understand.

Their whispers sounds like buzzing bees around his sleeping ears. "Don't use the ideas and words of people to find out who you are. It might not be the truth. Going without is not the answer. You need to go within."

They continue to dance and dart around him just as they did with Mthisa, and countless others before her. They know the only way Mandla can live the truth is by knowing the truth. There is nothing more they can do. He has to move out of the darkness into the light himself.

Closer than what Mandla realises a slender Sibongile is looking up at the moon. She can't shake the feeling that something is about to happen that will change her life forever. As she has done ever since she can remember, she wishes she had someone to talk to. There is so much her inquisitive mind doesn't understand.

Chapter 9
The Truth is Relentless

When Bongwe wakes up the sun has already started rising over the horizon announcing the start of a new day. He doesn't feel refreshed because he didn't have a good night sleep. Without having anything to eat he leaves his hut and heads to the nearby river.

By the time he gets there, he is out of breath and sweat is running in little rivers down his round face. His usual merry eyes are sombre when he bends down to drink from the river's cool refreshing water. Dewdrops tumble down on him from the low hanging branches of a willow tree when birds, nesting above, flap about protesting his presence.

Time has not been kind to him. He is still unmarried. Being overweight with a deformed arm is not exactly the making of a good catch. He gives a deep sigh, he was hoping the walk would clear the pain and memories that cloud and saturate his mind. "If only I can forget...........if only," he grunts.

An elegant giraffe walks towards the river. Momentarily distracted from his oppressive thoughts Bongwe watches her. "Imagine if I was a giraffe!" he thinks with envy. "I would be able to see further than any other animal or human. I could spend my days eating succulent leaves and have no concern about tomorrow. I won't care about what tomorrow may bring, and yesterday will be a fleeing memory that I waste no time on. Today will be the only day that counts. She doesn't know or care about her own death. She is content eating, mating and rearing her young. Even her dead body becomes a part from which others can feed and in turn survive." He shakes his head sadly. "My death will be marked by nothing. All that I will leave behind, if I should be so lucky, is just a memory in someone's mind."

In the tree above him the birds flap about noisily again causing a fresh shower of dewdrops. At the same time Bongwe notices Matsisi walking towards him. Surprised that Matsisi is up so early he calls out. "Matsisi! What are you doing here? Are you looking for me?" When Matsisi doesn't answer he walks closer. "Matsisi, what is it? Is something wrong?"

His eyes widen and all words instantly dry up in his mouth. The person in front of him looks like Matsisi, yet it is not! They both have the same athletic build, the same straight nose and broad shoulders. The only difference is the eyes. Matsisi has dark and brooding eyes while the eyes of the young man in front of him are sharp and penetrating.

Bongwe stares at him. He can't believe the strong resemblance to Matsisi. They could be twins! He staggers backwards with the implication of such a possibility. He even opens his mouth to speak but the words seem stuck in his throat.

Hesitantly he puts out his hand and touches Mandla's long hair hanging halfway down his back. He sucks his breath in sharply and jerks his hand back. For a wild moment he thought the person in front of him wasn't real. "Who are you?" he croaks while a thousand thoughts bounce through his head.

Mandla clears his throat. He is acutely aware of the shocked emotions flashing across Bongwe's face. "My name is Mandla,' he says. "I wonder if you can help me. I am looking for my family."

Bongwe's head spins and his legs feel like they can't carry the heavy weight anymore. "Yes certainly," he says with as much composure as he can manage. "Who are you looking for?"

"I am looking for a man called Thukani and his wife Lindiwi." Mandla answers.

Bongwe nods his head. "Yes, yes I know them. Are you related?"

Mandla hesitates. How much should he say? He feels a sudden rush through his body and knows without a doubt that he can trust this man in front of him with his life. He lifts his head and simply says. "They are my mother and father."

Bongwe feels like he wants to explode with excitement. Is it possible that the child left for the crocodile survived? Could it be? Dare he hope? Dare he! His huge stomach jumps up and down and he asks is a high voice. "Who raised you?"

"Mthisa." Mandla says simply.

Bongwe screams with delight. He steps forward and embraces the bemused Mandla. When he steps back tears are flowing down his round cheeks and he has a wide grin on his curved lips. He laughs and cries at the same time.

"Do you know me?" a very confused Mandla asks.

"Yes! Yes!" Bongwe almost screams. "I went to the river to look for you but thought you were dead. The same night I went to Mthisa but she wasn't there and no one ever saw her again. In the meantime she was obviously busy with other things," he rambles on. "Mthisa, Mthisa, the one seeing the unseen and knowing the unknown." Bongwe feels as if he has been given a second chance. He has so many questions he doesn't even know where to begin. He laughs delightfully when he remembers how Mthisa told him one day with flashing eyes. "We are all exactly where it is perfect for us to be!"

He gestures to Mandla to sit down on a fallen tree trunk. His eyes shine and sparkle. "I am Bongwe," he says. "Thukani and I have been friends since childhood. I know Mthisa as well, as much as anyone can ever know her," he prattles on.

Mandla sits down. His eyes never leave Bongwe's face and he drinks in every word. He doesn't want to miss anything, no matter how small. His fortunate accidental discovery of Bongwe confirms that everything is important, even a speck of dust.

Their conversation flows smooth and fluent. They tell each other everything. They receive answers to questions that lay in turmoil between their thoughts. At last they know how the broken pieces fit together. A deep understanding develops between them rapidly. A simple knowing that doesn't come from the mind but from the heart. They talk for a long time. There is much to say.

When all that needed to be said, had been said, the giraffe Bongwe was looking at earlier, leave the acacia tree, where she has been using her long flexible tongue to rip the leaves from the branches, and walks gracefully towards them. She emits a low moan to attract their attention. She has chestnut brown blotches against a buff background, markings that blend with the dappled shadows of the tree branches. Her neck is beautiful, long and sensuous. On her head are four short, blunt, skin-covered horns, almost like a crown. Her keen sense of smell, hearing and sight is focused on the humans.

Bongwe instinctively grabs Mandla's arm so he can pull him to safety. He feels unsafe so close to the giraffe. He has seen how giraffes can protect themselves by kicking with their large, heavy hooves.

Mandla shakes off his hand absentmindedly. He is not concerned. His eyes shine with admiration. He whispers softly to Bongwe so as not to scare her. "Only a genius could have designed and created such beauty. It is truly evidence of aesthetic flair. She is beautiful!"

The giraffe spreads her long forelegs wide and bends down in front of Mandla. Without fear he places his hand on her forehead. Their togetherness and their total oneness fill them. Mandla says gently. "Sometimes we find God in the most unexpected places."

Bongwe's mouth hangs open. He is totally amazed! He has never seen anything like this in his life! When the giraffe slowly straightens up and walks away gracefully, Bongwe knows that his life will never be the same again!

As they discussed and arranged, Bongwe returns to the village without Mandla. They both felt it would be better that Bongwe breaks the news to Thukani and Matsisi first before they meet Mandla. Even though Bongwe knows them both well he is decidedly unsure of their reaction.

Thukani is sitting in his usual place under the marula tree. He stares into the fire with hunched shoulders. His eyes, which used to be bright and intense, now sit deep and dark within his skull. It makes his slightly hooked nose more pronounced. His mouth, which rarely smiled anyway, is set in a grim unpleasant looking line. He doesn't walk often but when he does, it is with a limp, leaning to the left from his torso up. It is his constant reminder of the fateful day Shaka's armies wiped out what used to be their home. He is lost within his own thoughts in a place where no one has entrance, not even his best friend. He sleeps little because nightmares plague him. Unstoppable images constantly torture him. They fill his being so totally that it is all there is. It leaves him so empty and bare that he simply sits in the shade while life steadily flows by. He lives in the past and the future doesn't exist for him.

Bongwe looks at his friend. It breaks his heart to see him like this. He knows Thukani's spirit is as broken as his body. A wise old man once told him that your life is not about what your body is doing. Yet your body is always a reflection of what your life is about. He touches Thukani on the shoulder to draw him out of his morose mood. When Thukani looks up at him he says. "I have something important to tell you."

"Nothing is important anymore." Thukani answers in a flat voice.

Bongwe sits down. "Some things are my friend, some things are." He spots Matsisi and immediately calls to him. "Matsisi! Come here I have some important news!"

With some reluctance Matsisi walks over and kicks at a chicken that dared to cross his path. Following close to his heel is a dog. It is a large, shorthaired, black and brown spotted male with a broad forehead and face. It is Dumisai, his constant companion. He gives his father a disdainful look and sits down without greeting anyone. Dumisai growls deep within his throat at Thukani. Matsisi puts his hand on the dog's head. "Be still Dumisai!" he says sharply, but not before amusement sparkles in his eyes.

Bongwe feels shivers run up and down his spine when he looks at the dog. He hates those glinting dark eyes and needle sharp teeth. He looks away and clears his throat. "I met someone very important today."

Matsisi looks up and shows an immediate interest. It is always useful to know important people. He is unaware of the striking resembles between him and his twin brother.

Bongwe starts to stutter nervously. He meant to do this in a gentle and easy manner and now that the moment has arrived, all his carefully rehearsed words seem stuck in his throat. He simply blurts out. "I met this young man.............. his name is Mandla and. .... and........ and ....well, he's Matsisi's brother."

Matsisi raise his eyebrows. "I have no brother, you should know that, or don't you," he says sarcastically and roll his eyes. Bongwe is such a stupid old man.

With a deathly pale face Thukani struggle to his feet. "What are you talking about Bongwe?" he asks through tight lips.

The rest of Bongwe's words bust out. "Matsisi's twin brother is alive! Mthisa took him and raised him. Now he's come back! He's here and he wants to meet you!"

Slowly Thukani sinks down again with a body shaken to the core. He puts his head in his hands and as quickly as he left his safe inner impenetrable place he returns to it.

Matsisi ignores his father and looks at Bongwe darkly. He is not impressed. "How sure are you this man is my brother? How do you know he's not an imposter?" he hisses.

"I'm sure, I'm very sure!" Bongwe says in a bit of a high voice. "I've never been surer of anything in my life. He looks just like you. It is your brother!"

Matsisi gets up, gives Bongwe a tight factious grin and says, "Then we will welcome him!" He turns on his heels and walks away with Dumisai closely following. His jaw is clenched and his eyes shine with a kind of reckless wildness.

Sibongile hands Bongwe something to drink and sits down beside him. She doesn't offer anything to the silent Thukani. She knows he is lost in his own world. She is taller than any of the other women in the village. Her cheekbones are quite high and she has a slightly smaller version of her father's hooked nose. She is still single in spite of her attractiveness, and it could be because she has an unmistakable air of authority around her.

Just as Thukani is lost in his own thoughts, so are his lifelong friend Bongwe, and his oldest daughter Sibongile.

The ever-observant Sibongile watched and listened with interest to the conversation between Bongwe, Thukani and her half brother Matsisi. As she has always done since she was a little girl, she took advantage of her position as the oldest daughter of his First Wife to listen to serious discussions.

Her thoughts jump between past events with lightning speed trying to find some sense in it all. How often has she seen in her mind how the crocodile grabbed the helpless infant with a clenched jaw and drag him into the river? What a horrible way to die while the crocodile rolls and turns creating a turmoil of blood and mud to make sure his prey is dead and soft enough to eat. Maybe if Thukani weren't so selfish and left his own son at the mercy of a crocodile Shaka's armies wouldn't have attacked them?

So many people died that day. Smangaliso's warning was ignored and they paid for it dearly. The big man with the clean-shaven head and expressionless face fought bravely but his warriors didn't stand a chance against the swift, deadly and organized army. In the end the brave warrior gave his life to save her and Matsisi.

Lindiwi died as spear entered her heart. It is like the deadly accurate spear finished off what Thukani had started when he broke her heart. Did anymore mourn her death? Sibongile doesn't know. Even in death a descendant of Nzunza didn't gain the respect of the Manala people. At least her mother was buried with the respect appropriate of the First Wife.

She gives a deep sigh and asks Bongwe. "Do you think the Great Spirit is punishing us?"

Bongwe shakes his head. "I don't know," he says. "All I know is that the truth is relentless. It never leaves you alone. Just when you think you have moved away from it, it comes back. It creeps up on you from every side when you least expect it. It constantly annoys you until you cannot ignore it anymore." He looks over to the silent Thukani who is wiping over his face with a shaking hand. "Yes that's the problem with truth."

Sibongile nods her head and the burden she is carrying feels even heavier. So the shooting star she saw did have meaning! All they can do now is wait, and waiting can be just as painful as memories.

While everyone in the group is lost in their own thoughts, Matsisi heads for Effa's hut. He doesn't care that he looks exactly like this supposed brother. As far as he is concerned, he and only he, is the chosen one. When he reaches her hut he enters rudely without asking permission.

The plump middle-aged Effa looks up when he enters and sucks her breath in nervously when she sees it is Matsisi. She always feels as if her air supply gets cut off when Matsisi and his nasty dog is around.

Matsisi sits down uninvited and barks. "Tell me the story of my birth!" Dumisai sniffs around the hut and he calls him to his side. The dog flops down next to him. He is content for now having his master's loving hand on his head.

Effa looks at Matsisi and his dog through veiled eyes. She feels the anger build up inside her and for a wild moment considers telling him to go and kill himself. Maybe then she'll be rid of him! She puts her hand to her throat and swallows hard. It could cost her, her life!

She takes a deep breath and composes herself, once more resigned to the inevitable. As Nyathela's daughter she knows all the intricate details regarding the birth of the twins, hence Matsisi's constant visits to her. She clears her throat and starts telling Matsisi a story that he knows by heart. She keeps her eyes downcast so that she won't see his pleasure or be any part thereof. She obeys simply because she has no choice. He is Thukani's heir and future chief!

Matsisi's eyes are glued to her face. He drinks in every word. When she stops talking he gets up and walks out without a words of thanks or acknowledgement. His eyes shine and his own importance swells in his chest. He nods his head. It has just been confirmed again! He is the special and chosen one of the people. He will continue to demonstrate who he is and remind others of who they are.

Effa breathes a deep sigh of relief. She grabs the cornmeal beer hidden in the corner and drink deeply. She wipes her mouth with the back of her hand and mutters. "May the Great Spirit help us all!"

Chapter 10
Powerful Thoughts cause Powerful Actions

Mandla is on his way to the village. In the river he sees a crocodile basking in the morning sun and shivers. His parents gave him so willingly to the terror whose eyes shine red in the moonlight. He shakes his shoulders to get rid of the oppressive thought and tries to focus on how his family will react to meeting him. That doesn't really help either.

As he enters the village the first thing he notices is that it is very quiet. In his home village busy women will be painting huts, or helping hunters prepare meat and skin after a hunt. The quietness unsettles him bit, but he lifts his head proudly and pulls back his broad shoulders. As long as he is not too attached to results there is nothing to be afraid off. Whatever happens he will deal with it.

Unbeknown to Mandla the whole village has in fact come to an absolute standstill. The news of his unexpected arrival spread like wildfire last night and everyone is determined to see him. Excitement suppressed by fear, can create a strange mood.

In the doorways of huts silent people stare at him as he walks past. Some of the younger girls draw in their breaths as they see his athletic body and graceful walk. He looks like Matsisi but he radiates a certain something that Matsisi doesn't have. What could it be? The long hair or the broad shoulders, or maybe it is the aura of mystic?

They don't know, but give a deep sigh and roll their eyes towards the sky. Yes, he could make quite a husband!

Bongwe calls out to Mandla and with relief he heads towards him. He walks faster. He wants to get away from the uncomfortable stares of the villagers.

In a gesture of welcome Bongwe puts his one arm across Mandla's shoulders and ushers him unceremoniously inside Thukani's hut.

Inside Thukani struggles to his feet. His leg doesn't want to function after sitting still for so long. He doesn't say a word but his breathing has become a bit uneven. What a striking resemblance! He fights the temptation to lose himself in his inner world.

Bongwe performs the introductions, if one can call it introductions, because each one knows exactly who the other is.

Matsisi gets up reluctantly and frowns when Dumisai doesn't react with his usual growling at strangers. He allows himself a small nod of the head to acknowledge Mandla and sits down again.

Upon Bongwe's invitation Mandla sits down as well and as he does so he takes an unobtrusive deep breath. The atmosphere is uncomfortable and it is obvious no one knows what to say. He is acutely aware of the dark and brooding look of his brother. The triangle on his hip begins to burn and with it comes a measure of inner calm. He needs to be patient. Each one of them will have to try and untangle the series of events that brought them together before any conversation can begin.

Unexpectedly Matsisi jumps up with a clenched jaw. "I hope you don't think you can come here and claim what's rightfully mine!" he says in an aggressive tone.

Mandla's stomach contracts with tension. Looking at his brother is like looking at oneself in the clear still waters of a lake, but that's where the resemblance ends. "It was never my intension to claim something that doesn't belong to me. I simply wanted to meet my family," he says as calmly as he can.

Matsisi throws his arms in the air. "And you expect me to believe that!"

Mandla forces down his irritation at his brother's angry reaction. "I don't expect anything, except maybe that you try and understand."

Matsisi, who never had much self-control anyway, releases the anger that has been brooding inside him since last night. His hard mouth pulls downward and his voice is harsh and ugly. "There is one only thing that I understand, and that is that you're not wanted here! We don't want to see you. We don't want to meet you. In fact we want nothing to do with you at all. That is why I was chosen and not you! It will be better for all of us if you just leave and never come back! You are as unwanted now as you were the day you were born!"

Mandla jumps up and his eyes flash as darkly as his hostile twin brother's. "No! I will not skulk in the bushes. I will not try and hide who I am! I am the son of Thukani and Lindiwi, just as you are," he says with all the strength he can muster. He will not be intimidated by anyone.

Bongwe has also jumped to his feet. His looks dart from one young man to the other. He doesn't know how to defuse the explosive situation. All he knows is that he has to do something. Mandla doesn't know what Matsisi is capable off. He takes a step forward but stops when Dumisai growls from deep within his throat barring his yellow teeth.

Matsisi steps forward, pushes his face into Mandla's and hisses. "If you know what's good for you, you'll leave!"

Mandla returns Matsisi's cold look without blinking. His mind wields his muscles tight. He will stand his ground with solid energy.

Matsisi throws his head back and gives a wild hysterical laugh that makes Bongwe wince. He pretends to back away but jerks a knife from his belt of pushes it into Mandla's neck. With an ugly grin he pushes the knife deeper until a small stream of blood starts flowing past the sharp point of the knife.

Mandla feels the knifepoint cut even deeper into his skin. His birthmark starts burning at the same time and he feels a current of energy shoot through his body. It is a strange sensation yet it seems to calm his mind, body and emotions. He became so immersed in his anger that he forgot the true purpose of his mission. He gives a small smile. Sometimes we think we're normal because we all do the same thing.

Matsisi's disdainful look is replaced with disappointment Mandla's reaction. Unsure of what to do he keeps the knife at Mandla's neck but doesn't push it any deeper. He was hoping for a cringing coward not a calm expression and humorous smile! He winces when Mandla's iron grip enfolds his hand and forces the knife away from his neck. With bravado he keeps his eyes locked with Mandla and tries to push the knife back. He cannot, Mandla is too strong!

Without even a slight tremor in his voice Mandla says. "There are only two things that motivate men. The one is fear and the other one is love. Which one would apply to you my brother?"

Matsisi grinds his teeth and glares at his brother. He still cannot release his own hand from Mandla's firm grip. He utters a cry of rage. "What makes you think I'm afraid of you?" I fear no one! You hear me, no one!" He jerks his hand out of Mandla's and storms out of the hut. His anger towards the imposter, calling himself his brother, becomes even stronger.

Dumisai scuttles to his feet to follow his master. In his hurry, the large dog noisily scatters utensils in all directions.

Bongwe sinks down. He legs feel weak underneath his overweight body. He doesn't know what to say to Mandla, his thoughts are a scattered mess.

Thukani also breathes a sigh of relief. His twin sons flashing eyes has kept him rooted, unable to recede to his inner hiding place. He clears his throat and an ever so faint glimmer of accepting present reality peeps out. "Mandla, ...I'm sorry................... What Matsisi did is unacceptable........... I ...... I mean we..........."

Mandla interrupts him softly. "Don't apologize. Each one of us is responsible for our own actions."

Thukani shakes his head. The painful wound that he has been trying to heal is open and festering again. As fast as he can, he moves to his special safe and impenetrable place.

A silence, even more uncomfortable than before, is broken when the slender Sibongile enters and offers them refreshments. Bongwe hurries to introduce her to Mandla and she gives him a warm and welcome smile. Her eyes are clear and bright and on her head she is wearing a bright head cloth. She had taken extra care dressing today and she presents a well-groomed, neat, tidy and elegant lady.

Mandla immediately likes his slender half sister. What a pleasant surprise after the morose Thukani and angry Matsisi!

Against what custom demands she sits down beside them. In her usual direct manner she says to Mandla. "There is no excuse for my brother's behaviour but........." She sadly looks at her silent father, "As you never had a father to guide and help you, Matsisi didn't have one either." She turns back to Mandla. "I tried to be there for him when I could but being a young girl myself, I could never be a mother to him. He could pretty much do as he wished from the day he was born." She puts her hand on Mandla's knee as if she wants to enforce the importance of what she is saying. I know sometimes he acts in a horrible way but it is only because his actions are influenced by his thoughts."

Mandla looks at Sibongile, surprised by her unexpected wisdom. "I understand," he says. "Powerful thoughts can cause powerful actions."

Sibongile nods her head and gives a relieved smile. Could it be that Mandla holds the key to answers she is seeking? She certainly hopes so!

Determined to make up for Matsisi and Thukani's behaviour Bongwe offers Mandla his own home. He makes a point of mentioning that Mandla could stay there for as long as he likes. He can hardly conceal his delight when Mandla accepts. Matsisi had forbidden a feast in the village celebrating the arrival of Mandla and it irritates Bongwe immensely. He understands that a full-blown feast might be uncomfortable for some of the people, but the least Matsisi and Thukani could do was be a bit more welcoming.

They make their customary thanks to Sibongile and Thukani before leaving. Sibongile accepts with grace but Thukani doesn't respond, as usual he is in his own inner world.

Much later that night after sharing a meal with Bongwe, Mandla lies down to sleep. It has been a long and emotionally draining day. He closes his eyes and makes an effort to still the thoughts that jump around in his head. Soon he drifts off into the nothingness only sleep can bring.

While the moon rises higher and higher in the sky creating yet another night, the Spirit People come out. They giggle as some people pull their blankets over their heads to try and hide from the dancing shadows in the moonlight.

Earth people can be so strange. They think the Spirit People live only at night. They are wrong! The Spirit People are always there. It's just that during moon time they like to dance on the moonbeams, play in the shadows and catch a ride on the shooting stars. It is also the time when they sprinkle moon dust in people's eyes to let them dream. Sometimes of things to come, sometimes of things that have passed, and sometimes of things they need to understand.

Mandla, the son of Thukani, is also having a dream tonight, a strange dream. One that he would rather not have had, that is if he had anything to say about it, which he did not.

He dreams of two very large beasts, they are bigger than an elephant and taller than a giraffe. They have dry scaly skins with clawed feet. On top of their heads they have a single horn. Their mouths are full of vicious looking teeth, much like that of a crocodile. Trailing behind their large bodies is a long tail, like that of a fat lizard, with sharp protruding fins. One beast is black and the other one white.

The white one walks only during the day. He emerges only once the sun had risen in the east. While awake, it aggressively eats every tree in its path. It destroys as far as the eye can see. The beast grows stronger and stronger as it eats the trees. When the sun sets, the white beast lays down to rest.

As the moon rises the black beast awakens. It follows the same trail of the white beast but doesn't eat the trees. Instead it spits into each hole a tiny seed. He replaces diligently all the trees the white beast had destroyed. He toils long and hard and when the moon sets, marking the end of dark time, he goes to sleep.

The two beasts never see each other, until one day when their cycle gets interrupted by the sun and moon meeting. The sun is still setting but the moon is already visible in the sky. It is neither day nor night.

The beasts glare at each other with red angry eyes. The white beast gives an ear splitting high-pitched screech and inflates his lungs with air pretending to increase his size. The black beast growls deep within his throat and lunge forward as quick as he can attacking the white beast. They bite, claw, scratch and screech with only one object in mind, and that is to destroy each other.

Their battle continues throughout the night and the following day. Then they stop, unable to continue. Their bodies shiver and shake with exhaustion. Neither had won as both were of equal strength. The beasts had fought a battle with no outcome. They were exactly where they started!

The sky opens above them and two bright beams stream down. One covers the white beast and one the black beast. It starts lifting the beasts off the ground as if they are as light as feathers. They screech, complain and thrash about but are unable to escape. The beams hold them prisoner.

It moves them closer and closer together until they touch and begin to merge. They bite and claw in the brightness of the beam that blinds them, but it makes no difference. Only once they have merged into each another and become one, does the two beams leave.

In the place of the two beasts, there is now only one. The newly formed beast looks the same as before except its colour. It is now light grey. It is neither black nor white.

The fight for survival of each individual beast, now imprisoned into one body continues. Except now it becomes an inner fight. Now it is a mind fighting a mind. The body doesn't know who to obey and lies down. Still and shivering it will wait for death. The beast now knows, that the body is sustained by the mind. It is the mind that is the wielder of muscles.

A sleepy Mandla opens his eyes and makes a mental note to remember his dream. His heavy eyelids close again and the thought is lost. The Spirit People might have to remind him of the dream at a later stage.

Chapter 11

What you are Thinking you are Creating

Mandla is taking his usual walk after breakfast. There is a small smile on his lips and he breathes deeply of the fresh crisp air. He feels better this morning after the intense feelings of meeting his family yesterday. There's a lot he still has to learn and understand about his family, and things didn't go quite the way he had intended. Hopefully the lovely Sibongile and friendly Bongwe will be helpful.

A thought niggles in his head about a dream he had during his somewhat restless night, but it is pushed to the background when an agonizing scream fills the air. Immediately tense and alert his hand closes over the knife on his belt. The pain filled scream rips through the bushes around him a second time, and without hesitation he runs towards the open clearing where it is coming from.

Inside the clearing a young man is tied to a tree. His arms are stretched around its trunk and his hands tied together. His feet are bound together as well making movement virtually impossible. His back is covered with raw and open criss-cross wounds from which the blood runs freely. The rough bark of the tree has cut and bruised his haggard young face as he twisted and turned to try and free himself. His breathing is loud, hoarse and uneven. His whole body shivers and shakes with the effort.

Mandla rushes forward to untie him but jerks to a halt and swings around when Matsisi gives a wild, high laugh behind him. His eyes open in horror and the blood flowing in his veins turn to ice when he sees the bloodstained whip in Matsisi's hands.

Matsisi grins. "Do you like my whip?" he preens. "I got the best whip maker in the village to braid it for me. He lifts the whip into the air to look at it. "He made it from hippopotamus skin you know," he says with a glint in his eyes. He shakes his head in feigned sadness. "Sometimes we had to speak very harshly to whip maker before we were satisfied." He looks at his dog gnawing on the rope around his neck and says. "Didn't we Dumisai?"

He lets the whip run through his fingers. He loves to feel its texture and strokes it like one would a lover. "It's magnificent isn't it?" he asks Mandla without expecting an answer. How can Mandla possibly understand that his whip can bring pleasure and pain at the same time? Animated and excited by the thought he jerks his arm backwards and forwards in one smooth movement. The whip curls and snakes through the air. The villain snipes forward and greedily rips another piece of flesh from its victim's back. The young man screams in pain. Dumisai barks and jerks at the rope around his neck wildly.

Mandla feels sick to the pit of his stomach. He jumps in front of Matsisi and yells. "Stop! You'll kill him!"

Matsisi gives another high-pitched laugh. "That's the whole idea. I'm punishing him!"

124

"Are you mad!" Mandla shouts." What did he do to deserve such a harsh punishment?"

"He allowed the lions to feast on my cattle!" Matsisi screeches in a high voice. "A deed, that I have decided, as headman of the village, is punishable by a slow and painful death!"

Mandla shakes his head in disgust as he looks at the apparition representing his brother. A blood spluttered cough and low moan from the tree spurs him into action. With a tight mouth and dark eyes he runs towards the tree and starts cutting the leather strips binding the young man. He can't allow this torture to go on a moment longer!

Matsisi is furious. How dare his brother interfere in his business! He lifts his whip and it snakes forward to rip into Mandla's flesh.

Mandla drops his knife, sucks in his breath sharply, slumps forward and groans. He has never known anything to be so painful! The intense emotion of anger dulls the pain and he gets up slowly. When he turns towards Matsisi his eyes are as cold and hard as his brother's. With lightning speed he jerks the whip out of Matsisi's hand and throws it into the bushes. He picks up his knife and continues cutting away the bonds of Matsisi's prisoner.

Matsisi rushes forwards and grabs Mandla's arm. "You'll pay for this!" he hisses darkly.

Mandla jerks his arm away and continues cutting. When the young man crumbles to the ground he turns to Matsisi and says in an icy voice. "I will not allow you to treat anyone so cruelly!"

At his words Matsisi's face becomes a mask of fury. He jerks his knife from his belt and storms Mandla. He staggers backwards when

Mandla hits him in the face and with a raw scream of rage storms again. They fall to the ground while dust and leaves scatter around them. Two brothers, once safe and loved in the same womb, have become bitter enemies. A crested barbet lets out a long, sustained trilling "Trrrrrrr," but neither of them notices.

Mandla's eyes and heart are cold and hard. All the build-up anger, resentment and frustration explode through his fists, like lightning that has found a place to strike. His mind becomes the wielder of his muscles and he channels it with the force of a hammer blow. He doesn't try to stop it, he can't! It is unstoppable! He continues until Matsisi crumbles in a heap of bruises, blood and bitter surrender. He steps back and wipes the blood from his mouth with the back of his hand. His breathing is heavy and uneven.

With an expressionless face he watches a young woman run from the bushes towards the beaten and injured young man. She glances nervously at the unconscious Matsisi and wildly barking Dumisai. Determined to use the opportunity she puts her shoulder under the young man's arm and half drags, half carries him away. Before disappearing in the bushes she turns around and gives Mandla a grateful nod. Unresponsive his empty look stays the same. His anger had enveloped him like a hard shell and set him apart from anything else. Slowly he turns around and walks away.

At the river's edge Mandla walks into the water. His bruised and battered body is caked with blood, some of which is his own and some of which is not. He walks deeper and deeper into the river until he is totally submerged. He stays under the water till his lungs feel as if they want to burst. He comes up with a gasp only to fill his lungs and submerge again. It is almost as if staying under the water will help erase the horrible knowledge of what he has just done. He lets out his breath under the water and the air bubbles drift to the top. Some of the tension in his body seems to dissipate.

At long last he emerges and walks over to a willow tree. He sits down with his back against the tree and closes his eyes. He is weary beyond anything he has ever known. He frowns with irritation when his birthmark starts burning. He keeps his eyes closed and resist the temptation to rub it. How he hates it when it feels like someone is pushing a burning branch into it! His eyes fly open when he hears a slithering sound next to him. He sucks in his breath. It is a black mamba!

The snake lifts its narrow head, with its relatively large eyes, and looks at Mandla. It is black and slender with large scales and long venomous front teeth for paralysing its prey.

Mandla keeps dead still. He doesn't even want to blink his eyes. The dangerous black mamba can move at high speed and is extremely foul tempered. To the left and right of him two more mambas appear enclosing him in a triangle of snakes. The snakes raise the front of their long bodies into the air. Their forked tongues slide in and out while they move rhythmically from side to side as if they are dancing. A light wind is blowing and one could be made to believe that the wind is causing their hypnotic movements.

Mandla feels the pulling sensation in the centre of his forehead. He knows it is pointless to resists so he doesn't, but his thoughts are as bad tempered and black as the mambas.

The sun becomes brighter. It opens and three sparkling yellow sunbeams are born. They are much brighter than the moonbeams and Mandla shields his eyes from the strong glare. They form a triangle and drift down to earth. They shiver and glitter and settle around him with a mamba on each point.

The mambas stop moving and glow like they are filled with the sun. There is no movement except the heat waves that dance energetically on the sunbeams. The great stillness that surrounds the time warp the sunbeams created is broken by a clear distinct voice. "Everything that is, is alive."

Tanua appears and his longish clay white hair, with the bright red stripes, flutters in a wind that seems to surround only him. His green eyes sparkle and flash as he speaks again. "Everything that is, is alive. And you Mandla, are you alive?"

"Of course I am!" Mandla snaps and jumps up. "I'm here aren't I?"

Tanua lifts his eyebrows ever so slightly at Mandla's reaction. "That is not what I meant," he says calmly. "I mean do you understand that it's not only your body that's alive, your thoughts, emotions, and feelings are also alive."

Mandla doesn't answer. He knows too well how the intensity of his feelings and thoughts caused him to react.

"You are the same as your brother." Tanua says.

"No I am not!" Mandla denies with flashing eyes. "I am not like my brother. He is everything I am not!"

"Are you not Mandla?" Tanua asks. "Did you not a moment ago beat your brother into a bloodied mess? Did you not a while ago allow your anger and resentment to be released through your fists? Did you not do all that and much more? I tell you Mandla, you are exactly like your brother!"

Mandla sits down again and wipes his hand over his face. The truth is almost too much to bear. "No ......no..." he groans and shakes his head, "If that is so, that I am like him, I will do everything in my power to change."

"So you want to change because your brother is wrong and you are right?" Tanua asks.

Mandla nods his head. His eyes are dark and full of pain.

Tanua shakes his head. "There are no rights or wrongs in God's world. You don't have to agree with the way your brother treats people. In fact you cannot feel or think on his behalf. He doesn't see his actions as wrong because it is an accurate statement of who he is. Concern yourself only with what would make an accurate statement of your own life. Then seek to change not because another is wrong but because it is not an accurate statement of who you are. You cannot determine anything by the actions and feelings of others, only in your own.

Remember the dream you had about the two beasts. They showed you how thoughts and feelings are alive in anyone. You can take the body and give it any form; the thoughts and feelings will remain the same. You can even take the body of two beings and merge it into one. Each one's thoughts and feelings will remain the same.

Everything you think and everything you do is a act of self-definition, but you cannot choose if there is nothing to choose from."

I know who I am because I have demonstrated that which I am not." Mandla says hoarsely.

"Yes Beloved." Tanua says and disappears with a blinding flash. Once more everything is as it was.

Mandla gives a tired sigh and leans back against the willow tree. Without being told he knows that he has just received the gift of understanding. More than that he also knows that whatever he is thinking, he is creating.

The tree lowers its branches around him as if it wants to protect him. He doesn't notice. His weary eyes are closed, unaware that he is creating balance within and balance without.

In the bushes, not far from Mandla, Sibongile lets out a big sigh of relief. She thought her heart was going to stop when she saw the black mambas. She rubs her eyes hard trying to clear her head and make sense of what she has just seen. With a quick glance at the apparent sleeping Mandla she turns around and sneaks away.

She is not as neatly dressed as usual, in fact she looks a bit dishevelled. Her hair is uncovered and her eyes frightened. She ran as fast as she could when news of the fight reached the village but when she got there, the only evidence that remained was wet blood, cut leather strips, scattered leaves and dust trying to settle.

Following her instinct she headed for the river only to stumble upon Mandla, surrounded by snakes, and having a conversation with who knows what! Keeping her head down she continues walking in no direction. Thoughts spin and twirl in her head as she tries to understand. She feels as if she has lost all sense of what is real and what is not.

Suddenly she stops and looks up at the sky. Time stops for a moment in her own inner world. She whispers under her breath. "Matsisi and Mandla are both tall and well built, in fact exact duplicates of one another. Their bodies might be the same but their emotions and feelings are what make them different. Imagine if they both felt the same way!" She nods her head. "I think it is their differences that is going to save us."

Chapter 12
The Truth is Useless unless you Act upon it

Mandla walks into the village. He feels as if everyone is watching him. It is obvious that the news of what happened between him and Matsisi has already spread. "Dear God," he groans when he sees the sparkle in their eyes. "They respect me because I've beaten up my brother. They admire what I've done!" He increases his pace. Between him and Bongwe's hut his guilt lies like a mountain.

Bongwe is preparing a midday meal when he enters. He looks up and greets Mandla but continues to prepare the meal. He has learned that it is sometimes better to say nothing.

Mandla sits down. He watches Bongwe for a while trying to be patient but bursts out instead. "Where's Matsisi?"

"He has left in search of a lion that killed his cattle. Rather in a hurry it seemed and wasn't feeling too well by the look of things either." Bongwe answers with a chuckle and a small smile on his curved lips. He busily continues with the important task of preparing a meal.

Mandla jumps up and scowls. "I'm not proud of what I've done, you know!"

"No, Mandla, I don't suppose you are." Bongwe says and stops working. The look on his face becomes serious and intense at the same time. "What has happened though, is that you've given us new hope. For too long everyone in this village has been at the receiving end of Matsisi's brutality and anger. They didn't know what to do because the wrong decision could cost them their lives."

Mandla shakes his head. "It is not my place to stop him Bongwe."

"Yes but if you don't who will?" Bongwe asks. "The only other person that could possible do so is Thukani, but he lives in his own little world and no one knows if he's even aware of what's happening.

Mandla gives a deep sigh and sits down. "So these people think that I am the answer to their problem," he says.

"Of course they do!" Bongwe says. "And who can blame them! You are the first person that has ever stood up to Matsisi."

Mandla jumps up. "Do you really think that just because I have beaten my brother senseless it will stop him abusing the villagers?"

"Maybe it won't stop him but it will make him think twice." Bongwe insists.

Mandla shakes his head. "No Bongwe it won't."

"What should we do then?" Bongwe asks, and when Mandla doesn't answer, he walks over to him, puts his hand on his shoulder and says in a tight voice. "Not knowing what to do is the worse kind of suffering there is."

Mandla rubs his hand over his face. "The villagers are trying to label me a saviour. They want to make me into something I am not. I'm not the one who can save them. They are the only ones who can save themselves."

"What's wrong with it if we see you as someone who can save us?" Bongwe asks. "Do you hate us so much that you would rather see us destroyed than to help us?"

Mandla jumps up and pulls his shoulders back. "No Bongwe I don't hate anyone! But surely you don't expect me to kill my brother so he can stop killing others?"

"No... no.... Of course not!" Bongwe says apologetically.

Mandla touches his birthmark when it starts burning. He frowns but gets distracted by a call outside asking for permission to enter.

Sibongile walks in through the door. She is well dressed and her hair neat and tidy. She acknowledges Mandla but keeps her eyes lowered as if she wants to hide her thoughts. Uncomfortably she sits down. Intuitively she knows what they have been talking about and wonders how to broach a subject she doesn't really want to talk about. She comes to a decision and proudly lifts her head. "All Matsisi ever wanted to do was to make our father proud. When Thukani didn't notice or care, he began hurting others as a way to relieve his own pain," she says a bit aggressively.

When neither Bongwe nor Mandla responds, she jumps up and confronts Mandla with fire in her dark eyes. "I am not making excuses for him! All I want is for you to understand why he is the way he is. We might not like what he does but he is still our brother!"

Mandla looks at her and says calmly. "Yes he is."

"What are you going to do?" she asks in a tight voice. There has been so much violence she doesn't know if she could bare anymore.

She clenches her firsts. How she wishes she wasn't a woman and could have more control over what happens in the village.

"I am not going to do anything," Mandla says. "The people are trying to make me into something that I am not. It will be better for them to concentrate on who they are rather than what they want me to be." Absentmindedly he rubs his burning birthmark, and continues talking almost as if he is working it out for himself. "Everyone has kept quiet. They have allowed Matsisi to do whatever he likes. They brought it into being by accepting it."

Sibongile eyes are glued to Mandla's face as she learns forward. "Do you mean that it is useless to know the truth if you don't do anything about it?"

Mandla nods his head and looks at her. "Yes! You can stop anything happening in your life by simply choosing to stop it happening."

"But we have tried to stop it!" Bongwe pips up. "We have even asked the Great Spirit for his help!"

Mandla gives a small smile. "Even if you ask the Great Spirit for help, you cannot be helped. You see Bongwe you have been sending two different messages. One is the feeling in your hearts that what is happening is wrong. The second one, from your mind, is that you need to accept what is happening because resistance would mean death. The Great Spirit listens but doesn't know which message to respond to."

"Our hearts know what the truth is." Sibongile says. "If we want to break the cycle we need to choose to do so." She frowns. "Can it really be so simple?"

"Yes Sibongile," Mandla says. "When you choose to act upon the truth anything is possible!"

"I don't understand," Bongwe says. What are we suppose to do?"

Sibongile gets up and walks towards the door. "We must talk to Matsisi and insist he stops his behaviour," she says. Bongwe's high voice of, "You're not serious!" follows her out the door. She pays no attention to it. There is much to be done. It will take at least two days to get everyone together. Her determined steps lead her to Thukani's hut first. She lifts her head proudly and pulls her slender form upright. "There is nothing she cannot be and nothing she cannot do!"

By midday a couple of days later, everyone in the village had finished their chores. Despite a restless night most of them were up early. The meeting today dominates everyone's thoughts. Dare they hope that Mandla can stop his brother? Or, are they simply replacing one tyrant for another? Most of them hold Thukani personally responsible for the whole mess, but will not dare to say so openly. They try to keep their restless minds busy, but the scorching sun and their strained emotions makes it too hard. Today is going to be a hot day in more ways than one!

Late afternoon, when it is cooler, the selected elders start arriving at the meeting place, a round cleared circle on the east side of the village. Inside, a couple of early arrivals are already settled on smooth and faded wooded seats. As more elders enter, a low hum can be heard as they talk among themselves. Most of them are tense and nervous. Hopefully Matsisi is still occupied with finding the lion that killed some of his cattle. No one seems to care whether Thukani is attending nor not.

A small group consisting of Sibongile, Bongwe, Mandla and Thukani wait patiently outside the fence of long wooden branches for the elders to be seated.

Sibongile takes the limping Thukani's arm and together they enter the meeting place. She ignores the indignant looks of some of the elders. "Their minds are as dry and lifeless as the wooden fence," she thinks to herself. Holding her head high she walks with her father and sits down next to him. She will no longer hide or stand back for anyone because she is a woman!

Mandla sits down next to Sibongile. He gives a small smile when he notices her arrogant look and flashing eyes. She will make an excellent leader!

Bongwe walks into the centre of the gathering and clears his throat. Everyone immediately becomes silent and attentive and Bongwe clears his throat again. His merry eyes are uncertain and he feels decidedly uncomfortable in the role he has to play today. He looks around awkwardly but after a nod of encouragement from Mandla he finds the courage to start.

He spends a bit of time on niceties, welcoming everyone and talking about unimportant matters like the weather and cattle. Aware of the impatient looks on the elders' faces he takes a deep breath and broaches the subject everyone is here for today. "According to our tradition Thukani's heir becomes our leader, and at birth Matsisi was chosen by the elders for this role. Unfortunately this choice has caused us nothing but pain. Matsisi seems to be possessed by some kind of madness where he is beating and killing our people. I'm sure you've all heard how he nearly beat Danisile's brother to death with his whip. We cannot allow this behaviour to continue any longer. We have to do something."

A rumble of excitement runs through the elders, could it be that they will be free of Matsisi's tyranny at last. Some look at Thukani with disgust. They are not responsible for the way Matsisi has turned out. The responsibility should be placed squarely on Thukani's shoulders.

An old man with a face pulled tight in anger jumps up and shouts with a bitter voice. "My only son was murdered by Matsisi and his men! I think we should kill him!" A woman shouts in a high and shrill voice. "He dishonoured my daughter the disgusting evil man!"

Like a river whose banks just burst, wild shouts of anger echo through the air. "He beat me with his whip and left me for dead! He killed my cattle! He burnt my hut to ashes! The small fearful voice pleading caution had become still and silent. It is dominated by resentment, unjust treatment and hatred.

Jabulani, a very respected elder, gets up and gestures to everyone to be quiet. His shoulders are hunched and his body is old and wrinkled. He speaks in a quivering voice, yet it demands immediate respect and attention. "There's not one of us who has not had first hand experience of Matsisi's abuse. It saddens me that someone like that is to be our future leader." He glances briefly at Thukani but there is no apology or respect in his eyes. " I believe even Thukani understands what needs to be done and I'm sure it fills him with the same pain as it does me. I agree with Bongwe. It's time for it to end. Matsisi needs to be killed!"

The elders jump to their feet and cheer. Those that cannot get up use their walking sticks and bang it against the wooden seats. They are thrilled and beside themselves with excitement.

Horrified Bongwe holds up arms trying to restore order. He did not for one moment imply or mean that Matsisi must be killed. He tries to speak but his words are lost amidst the noise.

Mandla's can't take it any longer. He jumps up and joins Bongwe. He feels as if all the hatred is choking him. He has to stop them now! He lifts up his hand indicating that he wants to speak and a relieved Bongwe steps back.

The crowd settles immediately. It is going to be very interesting to hear what Matsisi's, thought to be dead, brother has to say.

Mandla takes a deep breath. It is important that he remains calm with all his wits about him. He lifts his head and his piercing eyes scan the crowd for anyone who wants to challenge his right to speak. His muscles bulge with the effort and from nowhere a light gust of wind tangles around him. He shakes his head and his hair sways like a mane of a lion. When he starts talking the passion in his strong voice is unmistakable. " Killing is not a way to solve your problem. You will be murdering the person you hate, but it will not get rid of that hate that is in your hearts. Your anger and hatred surrounds you so completely that you are becoming what you are trying to destroy."

Speechless the elders look at Mandla. They shake their heads in disbelieve. To think that for a wild moment he reminded them of a strong Thukani that once stood before them.

Jabulani breaks the stunned silence by voicing their thoughts in his quivering voice. "I'm a bit confused young man. I seem to remember you nearly killed your brother yesterday, now you're telling us not to kill."

Unwaveringly Mandla returns his gaze. "Yes I did, and I'm not proud of it! It has however taught me a very valuable lesson. When you return violence for violence it only multiplies. Darkness cannot drive out darkness, only light can do that."

Jabulani replies with a sarcastic smirk on his age-old face. "Well, what exactly did you have in mind? Do you know of a better way to deal with Matsisi?"

Mandla shakes his head ignoring Jabulani's tone. "No, I don't know a better way, merely another way. I believe we should make a choice of peace rather than one of murder. I suggest we confront Matsisi and tell him to stop his abuse and killing or he'll be banished from the village."

The whole crowd looks at Mandla with wide eyes. "You're not serious!" Jabulani's croak reflects their disbelief.

"If you act in love and truth anything is possible." Mandla says calmly.

"Truth and love!" Jabulani growls and sits down shaking his head. Loud voices protest around him. What Mandla is proposing is unacceptable! They continue to shake their heads in disapproval, and without realizing it, their thoughts swirl like dust in a sandstorm and form a collective thought of hatred and murder.

A young, small and petite woman, with long neatly braided hair walks uninvited through the gates into the meeting place. She stops next to Mandla, gives him a curt nod and faces the elders.

Silence settles immediately and though surprised, no offence is taken at her unexpected entrance. The selected elders nod in approval, they are quite prepared to give her a chance to speak. After all was it not her brother that was half beaten to death with Matsisi's new whip. Besides that, they all know Danisile with the wide smile and soft eyes. Her slender hands have nursed many sick people to health and her infectious laughter has gladdened many hearts.

Her usual soft and gentle voice is surprisingly firm when she starts speaking. "You want to kill Matsisi to stop him killing. Do you honestly believe that it will solve our problem? Surely you realize that once Matsisi is killed, another will replace him, for that is the way you are thinking. Violence brings more violence and hatred fuels more hatred."

She stamps her little foot on the ground. "What in the name of the Great Sprit are you thinking off? Do you really want to teach our children that the way we solve our problems is by killing? You are showing them that for their own survival they must kill or otherwise they themselves will be killed. We cannot be lovable to our children one day and be murderers the next day. We are either one or the other."

She stops a bit out of breath and her usual wide smile is lost in her pleading eyes. "Are you so filled with hatred that you refuse to see that there is another way out? Put your thoughts of killing away for a moment and listen to the true feelings of your heart. What Mandla is suggesting, is the only way we can save ourselves without becoming murderers."

The following silence that greets Danisile's words is so big that one might almost believe that no one heard a word she said. It is only broken when Jabulani slowly struggles to his feet. He ignores Mandla and addresses Danisile instead. "You have spoken wisely child, not with the wisdom of the world but with the wisdom of the Great Spirit."

He nods his grey head and his frail frame shakes as he does so. "You are right, it is not our obligation to spend our time finding a way to kill Matsisi. It is a decision for the Great Spirit alone to make. He takes a deep breath and announces in a voice that will not accept resistance or argument. "Matsisi is to be banished from the village and never be allowed to return."

Bongwe breathes a deep sigh of relief and gives Mandla a quick look and small smile. If there is anyone that could convince the elders it is Danisile! What a stroke of luck that she turned up today. Everyone likes and trusts her and she has given off herself willingly more than anyone else he knows.

The elders start leaving the meeting place without challenging the influential Jabulani. It is obvious the decision is made whether they go along with it or not. Bitterness and anger is still visible amongst some as they murmur in soft voices. They walk past the still seated and silent Thukani but ignores him. He has become an empty vessel to them. He is nothing more than a dead spirit with a broken body waiting for death, whenever it may come. He contains nothing of value anymore.

The sun is setting and the moon is already visible in the sky but no one cares or notices. They are too busy suppressing their fear. Some things are better not to think about.

Chapter 13

Surrender to your Feelings

The atmosphere, that the combined glow of the sun and moon creates on the cleared round circle on the east side of the village, which serves as a meeting place, is almost eerie. Everyone has left except Sibongile and Thukani, who are still seated on one of the smooth and faded wooden seats.

Without realizing it Sibongile's chin is still lifted proudly and her eyes still have a defiant look. She's not in a hurry to leave, for now content to enjoy the still silence of the empty meeting place. A small smile curves her lips and a bubble of a laugh jumps out. She nods her head and her eyes glint with satisfaction. Everyone got the message loud and clear. She will not allow the elders, Matsisi, Thukani or anyone in the village to ignore her any longer!

Thukani grunts and her look change to one of concern. She puts her slender hand on his arm, "Are you ready to leave father?" she asks. Her eyebrows lift in surprise when an obviously irritated Thukani shakes her hand off his arm and struggle to his feet. He starts walking away from her with a limp leaning to the left from his torso up. It seems even more pronounced than usual, possibly from sitting still for too long.

He stops his laboured walk as suddenly as it began, turns around and looks at the still seated Sibongile. "I have not been a good father to Matsisi," he says in a broken voice. She opens her mouth to protest but he gestures to her to be quiet. "I have also not been a very good leader to my people............. I can never ask them to forgive me.......... How can I? .... I can't even forgive myself."

Sibongile's mouth hangs open in amazement. She though he wasn't even aware of what happened at the meeting today. Yet his usual dull and lifeless eyes are bright and intense. A shiver runs down her spine when she sees glimpses of the old Thukani she remembers as a child.

"Have you ever hunted a buffalo?" he asks the dumbfounded Sibongile and continues without waiting for her reply. "One day I took my warriors to hunt a buffalo." His mouth pulls in a sarcastic smile. "I was so arrogant, all I cared about was that we were going to bring a large and powerful animal to its knees. I wanted the big horns, which are massive at the base and form a helmet over the buffalo's forehead, as a trophy to show how good I am. We walked for days until I found a buffalo magnificent enough to satisfy me. Eagerly we closed in for the kill but my pride wouldn't allow me to let my warriors help me. I wanted to kill the buffalo all by myself."

A bit out of breath he pauses. "I pulled back my spear and threw it with all my might, but instead of a smooth kill, all I did was wound the buffalo. For days we followed his bloodied trail, convinced that he will soon die from pain or exhaustion." He gives his sarcastic smile again. "How wrong I was! I never realized that the wounded buffalo was setting a trap for us. He was leading us to where he wanted us to go."

Thukani's looks up at the sky, his hooked nose more pronounced in the now near darkness. "Without warning the buffalo attacked us from behind with all the strength left in his body. He was willing to fight till his last breath.

We scattered in different directions, everyone only concerned with saving himself. Thukani gives a deep sigh. "After the brave Smangaliso, a large rock of a man and my head warrior, killed the buffalo, we stared speechless and in awe at the large lifeless animal. We never knew a buffalo could play the deadly game of revenge and we found out what it felt like to be hunted instead of being the hunter."

He looks at the confused Sibongile. "I have spent so much time hiding within myself that only now that my days are practically over, have I realize the truth. Matsisi is like a wounded buffalo. One that I have wounded myself." With that he turns and starts limping out of the meeting place.

Sibongile watches him go. She doesn't jump up to help him as she usually does. Something in his manner tells her it will not be accepted. She rubs her hand over her face. Could it be that Jabulani's angry words broke into her father's inner world? She shakes her head. Then again maybe it was Danisile's soft arrows that found a painful mark. She gives a deep sigh and looks up at the sky at the same time a shooting star leaves a bright tail in its wake. Slowly she gets up and walks away. Inside she feels tense and afraid. The last time she saw a shooting star her life changed. Is it about to change again?

The moon has become brighter and the Spirit People are playing with the wind in the treetops. They have jumped from the stars to come and play as they have done since the beginning of time. How they love twirling in the wind and playing hide and seek in the shadows.

They stop playing to follow Sibongile home. They watch her try to still her restless mind and sleep. They gather around her tossing and turning body and whisper in soft voices that everything will be just fine. They do the same with Thukani. He should know better than to think he's worth nothing. Every part depends on the other ensuring a delicate balance.

They continue dancing with all their hearts. The village is covered in an atmosphere of doom and heaviness and they are hoping that they can lift it. They dart to the little children reassuring them with silky soft sounds that creep into every crevice of their beings. They tickle their faces with feather light fingers till the little ones smile and start dreaming delightful dreams.

They stop only when the sun stretches lazily over the horizon. They take one last look at the village and disappear into the morning light.

Mandla gets up early and heads for the bushes as soon as he can. He didn't have a good night sleep and hopes that the fresh air will clear his head. The reason for his restless night is not the all-important meeting with the elders, but the stunning Danisile. How she impressed him with her wide smile, pleading eyes and wise words.

To his unexpected delight he sees her small frame half hidden in the long grass. Without any hesitation he heads in her direction. As he gets closer he notices she is cutting fresh herbs and tying them in little bundles. She hears his approach and jumps up with a look of fright on her face.

"Are the herbs for a brew to cure all the hearts you're breaking?" Mandla asks her in a playful voice. Her face loses its frightened look and a smile jumps into her eyes. She wipes the long braids out of her face and shakes her head. "No, I want to make a mixture for a bad cough."

"Mthisa taught me a lot about herbs," he says to her, "Would you like some help?" When she nods her head accepting his offer he bends down and starts helping her.

"Who is Mthisa?" she asks glancing sideways at him.

"A fierce little woman that can turn your world upside down in a instant!" he says with a groan.

"Your wife?" she asks.

He shakes his head. "No, I don't have a wife. Maybe you'll consider marrying me," he says with a glint in his eyes.

Her infectious laugh fills the air around them. "I think it will be better if you just stick to telling me about herbs."

Mandla gives a big sigh indicating that he accepts the rejection. "I will tell you about herbs then," he says in a flat voice.

Soon they are in a deep discussion concerning herbs. Mandla shares his vast knowledge of herbs while she makes mental notes to remember important information. When the sun is higher in the sky and it is too hot to cut herbs anymore, they stop.

Danisile gathers all the herb bundles and puts them in her bag. She turns to Mandla, says thank you in a bit of an out of breath voice and walks away.

Mandla's eyes follow her and the sensual sway of her hips takes his breath away. To Mandla it looks as if the sun's rays bouncing off her head are creating a halo of light around her. Soon she is out of sight and the space around him feels empty without her presence. His eyes however, have a new sparkle. Tomorrow is a new day with distinct possibilities.

A couple of days later Mandla wakes up with a fluttering heart. He was thinking about Danisile when he fell asleep and she is in his thoughts as he wakes up. He gets up, determined to find her again today. Her soft and gentle voice, infused with wisdom, passion and strength draws him like nothing he has ever experienced before. He knows then and there that he wants nothing more than to have her as part of his life.

As if fate is guiding his actions he heads towards the river. A big smile breaks the serious look on his face when he sees her. She is doing her washing. Her slender hands efficiently rub and rinse her clothes. He sucks in his breath. Even while performing such a simple task she is stunning.

Her hands stop their busy movement when she notices Mandla. She jumps up and wipes her wet hands over her braided hair and crumpled dress. "Have you come to help with the washing?" she asks in a light voice.

Mandla throws his head back and laughs. "No, I don't think so," he jokes back, "It is a woman's work."

She bends down, picks up a wet garment and throws it at him. It catches him by surprise and the water wets his dry clothes. With a grin he tosses it back and a childish game of throwing wet clothes at each other begins. It is not long before they are both soaking wet.

Out of breath they sink down on a patch of dry grass. They giggle like children and their eyes sparkle with excitement. An ordinary day is suddenly not so ordinary anymore!

The laughter dries up in Danisile throat and she blushes when she notices Mandla intent gaze on her. She opens her mouth to speak but any words that might have been there, dries up in her throat. Her heart starts thumping wildly when she sees the desire in his eyes. A shock shoots through her body when he lifts his hand and softly touches her cheek. She looks at him with wide eyes and cannot stop herself from drowning in the whirlpool of his presence.

Mandla feels the soft silky skin beneath his hand. Her red lips invite him closer and he leans forward and covers her soft sensual mouth with his. When he feels her respond, he pulls her closer into his embrace. When he stops kissing her, she whispers his name and it sounds like a musical instrument that has just made a beautiful sound.

With a groan her pulls her closer again, he feels as if he wants to pull her within his very being. He kisses her passionately and his head spins when she meets it with her own innocent passion.

Danisile jumps out of Mandla's embrace when some impalas, which were grazing behind them, scatter and run. She takes a deep breath and gets up to compose herself, but also to control her thumping heart. Without a word she starts gathering her wet clothes. Aware that Mandla is helping her collect the now dirty clothes she keeps her eyes downcast. Without a word she starts doing her washing again.

Mandla looks down at her with a tender smile. He bends down, lifts her chin with his hand, and gives her a light kiss before walking away. She bends her head again and continues washing, but not before he saw the small tug of a smile on her lips. Mandla grins, things are going well.

Danisile stops washing and turns her head to watch him walk away. He passes the nervous impalas. They are chestnut- brown above and white below with a distinctive black streak on each haunch. The males have graceful lyre shaped long black horns. They watch him leave while keeping a sharp lookout. If need be they will scatter again to confuse predators.

In the darkness the Spirit People come out to share the world of the Earth People They giggle when they look at Mandla and Danisile. Nothing can stop the couple from surrendering to their feelings. They become serious and settle down to disperse in different directions to do some healing. They can come back to Mandla and Danisile later. The couple needs to be alone for now. They are fulfilling a very important destiny.

In the days and nights that follow, Mandla and Danisile spend as much time as they can together. It is as if a strong magnet draws them closer and closer. They don't resist, instead they welcome and trust whatever their togetherness might reveal.

In the soft moonlight Mandla looks at Danisile's naked, silky shoulder and whispers. "I love you more than I ever knew it possible to love anyone." As if she hears him in her dream world she moves closer to him and he tightens his hold, loving her even more.

Mandla and Danisile has become one. They are wrapped within one another, one heart and one mind sharing the magnificence of total oneness. Their love is all there is now. For the lovers the world has stopped turning. The rotation of the earth is nothing compared to what they are feeling and each day becomes a lifetime.

With considerable reluctance they have to force themselves every now and then to become part of daily life again. They accept an invitation to share a meal with Bongwe, Thukani and Sibongile.

Sibongile made sure that the meal was prepared to perfection before she starts serving. She drops some food on her clothes and gets up with an irritated frown. As usual she has taken extra care dressing and her colourful head cloth matches the colour of her dress. She cleans the dirty spot and without wanting to, looks over to the Mandla and Danisile. When a special look, that only lovers share, pass between them she mumbles some excuse that no one pays attention to anyway, and rushes outside.

In the bright moonlight she squeezes her eyes tight to stop the tears. Mandla has become so much more than a brother to her. She has shared her dreams and fears with him, truly communicating, instead of just taking turns talking. She swings around in fright when she feels a hand on her shoulder. It is Bongwe.

His merry eyes are soft and caring but he doesn't say a word. He knows some things cannot be understood by the mind, only by the heart.

Sibongile gives him a sad smile, turns around and walk away with a heavy heart. She stops underneath the old maroela tree Thukani usually sits under. The wind breezes through the leaves making a soft sound but even that fail to calm her. With quick steps she continues walking till she comes to the village meeting place. She enters without hesitation. This is where she wants to be, where the space around her is open and uncluttered.

The same breeze starts playing around her feet and lifts the dust around her but she looks at it without emotion. Slowly Sibongile lifts her gaze up to the sky. "Please send me someone who will love me just as I am," she says in a broken voice.

The moon glows brighter and the stars flicker and glitter but Sibongile, the oldest daughter of Thukani, doesn't notice. Her hands are covering her face and her shoulders shakes from the sobs racking her body. Will she ever know the bliss of oneness with someone you love?

Chapter 14

The Burden of your Actions

In the village the world has stopped turning as well. They get up every morning and set about their daily tasks. They try not to think about Matsisi's imminent return and they certainly don't voice that they wish he would disappear into the blazing sun. No, tense and afraid they rather immerge themselves, as hard as they can, in the mundane things that are so consistent with daily life.

Then, one fateful day, as the first rooster crows, the world creaks and groans and spins their lives into action again. Word has reached the village Matsisi is on his way home!

In near panic mothers grab their children and secure them in the huts. Their eyes follow Sibongile's messengers, informing the elders that Matsisi's is on his way back to the village. In small groups they talk in lowered voices trying to find some comfort in each other's presence. What will this day bring? They don't know!

With slow steps, heavy hearts and sombre faces, the elders make their way to the meeting place. Conversation is limited to half-heated greetings and the atmosphere is filled with suspense. Are they scared of the decision that was made at the previous meeting? Yes indeed they are, even more so because they are so attached to the result of their decision.

As with the last meeting Thukani enters with Sibongile and Bongwe. Mandla and Danisile follow close behind. Without conversation they all take their seats and wait for Matsisi's arrival.

Matsisi walks into the village with a scowl and in a black mood. The long search for the lion that killed his cattle was unsuccessful.

His men make sure they walk behind him. They don't talk. It is better for someone else to get in his way. They don't want to bear the brunt of his anger!

A smirk jumps to Matsisi's face when he sees the villagers scatter. When he passes the meeting place and notices the elders gathered there, he stops dead in his tracks. He swings around and enters with an arrogant swing. "What's the meaning of this!" he barks.

When no one answers he grins at their cowardice. He deliberately lowers his hand and touches his whip. His sick grin widens when Dumisai, his vicious looking black dog, growls deep in his throat.

The elders look at each other. No one wants to start talking. In their eyes fear is so tangible, that you can almost touch it. They gasp in surprise when Thukani gets up and walks toward Matsisi with a difficult limp.

"I have called this meeting my son." Thukani says to Matsisi.

Matsisi is instantaneously furious. "How dare you be so insolent!" he hisses. "No meeting is called without the chief present!"

Thukani meets Matsisi's gaze without a flinch. "I am the chief Matsisi, not you."

"What!" Matsisi shouts.

"I am the chief," Thukani repeats in a clear voice. "You can only claim the honour of such a position when I hand it over to you, or lay down my head to die. Till then I am the chief."

Matsisi throws back his head and gives a wild, ugly laugh. He mockingly bows towards his father and says in a sick and forced sweet voice. "Oh my dear father, if it's your death you are seeking it can always be arranged. Besides, you're an old man with empty eyes, what possible threat are you to me? Nothing I tell you! It is as if you don't even exist, you never have!"

Matsisi's men, who are mostly loots and losers, snigger openly.

Thukani pulls his shoulders back and lifts his head. He doesn't say a word but his eyes, once dead and lifeless, are alive and bright. He gives Matsisi a piercing look.

Matsisi grin disappears and he frowns. He can't believe the defiant man standing in front of him is the old, weak and empty Thukani that he knows.

The elders gasp and look at each other with wide eyes. Thukani? Is that really you? They feel as if an ice cold wind just blew over them. Can it be? Dare they hope?

A stunned Sibongile and Bongwe look at each other and shake their heads in disbelief. Till a couple of moments ago Thukani had been his old self, sitting under his maroela tree while time slowly ticks by. The glimpse Sibongile saw of the old Thukani after the last meeting is nothing compared to the strong and confident man standing in front of Matsisi.

Thukani turns his back on Matsisi and addresses the elders. There is no hesitation in his firm voice. What he is doing today should have been done long ago. "Our struggle has been long and hard," he says. "After our village was destroyed by Shaka very little remained. Yet you, the elders of this village, pushed your pain aside and rebuilt from what little remained." He shakes his head. "I didn't help you. No........ I hid away......... trying to hide from the pain of defeat." He looks towards Sibongile and Bongwe briefly then back at the elders. "I beg your forgiveness my people, for deserting you when you needed me the most."

Thukani waits in silence for a while. He does so deliberately. Has he not always known how to deal with his people? "Today I have conquered the darkness. I am ready to lead my people and make the Ndebele people a great nation once more."

A cry rips through the crowd. Outside the meeting place, inquisitive villagers, who had been peering through the wooden poles with thumping hearts, jump up and down with joy. Every syllable of Thukani's words has been etched in their minds and hearts. It has happened at last! Thukani, also known as Isilwane, meaning lion, is back!"

Thukani bows his head in acceptance but at the same time hides a small satisfied smile. He lifts his head and gestures to everyone to be silent. Slowly he turns towards Matsisi. With undeniable authority he says. "My people have spoken about the way you treat them, and I have heard their words. It disgusted me and I am ashamed to call you my son and heir!"

158

Matsisi jerks his body upright and takes a threatening step towards his father.

Thukani continues as if he didn't notice. "Nothing we do in life is without repercussions. It is the law of the Great Spirit. I will carry the burden of deserting my people, in their time of need, for the rest of my life. You, my son, also have to take responsibility for your actions."

"I'll do whatever I want to do!" Matsisi shouts at his father. "Why don't you go back and sit under your tree like the dead-alive man you are!"

Thukani shakes his head. "One day I might long for the solitude of aloneness again, but today, I am chief of this village and its people." He takes a limping step towards Matsisi and Matsisi takes a step back away from the flashing dark eyes of his father.

"I have found that you have been without honour in your treatment of our people. You are therefore banished from the village. You, together with your followers, will leave the village before nightfall. You can never return."

Matsisi is numb with shock. He feels as if someone has just punched him in the stomach. He opens his mouth to speak but no words come out. All he is able to do is stare at his father. Thukani stares back and it becomes a timeless moment of unspoken words, containing a lifetime that lay still on their tongues.

Above them a fish eagle lets out a long dramatic lonesome call. Its piercing cry coincides with the violent anger that explodes within Matsisi. Bitter thoughts flash in his head. His whole life he tried to make his father proud but Thukani wasn't even aware of his existence. Now he has the audacity to banish him from his home and kingdom! How dare he!" His body is tense and taunt as he defiantly faces his father.

Thukani stands firm and fearless. Authority is written all over him.

Matsisi sucks in his breath sharply. The cool, yet piercing eyes of his father has just reminded him of his brother Mandla. His mouth pulls in a bitter line and the hatred for his father and brother burst within him like a violent thunderstorm. With uncontrollable rage he pushes his face into his father's and screams. "This is all because of Mandla isn't it? My so-called brother that came here under false pretences! You are too blind to see that he is deceiving you. He is using pretty tricks to make you believe he is better than I. He is nothing more than a skunk wallowing in its own stench!"

Mandla jumps up at the insult but Danisile grabs his arm and pulls him back.

Matsisi looks over to Mandla and screams at his men. "Bring him to me! I'm going to rid myself of him once and for all!" His men hurry to obey and drag a struggling Mandla over to him. He waits until they had forced Mandla to his knees then kicks him in the stomach as hard as he can. Before Mandla has time to recover he kicks him in the face.

Danisile screams and jumps up. Bongwe grabs her arm and pulls her down. She sits down quickly and puts her hand over her mouth, but it is too late. Matsisi has seen her. With wide eyes she watches his arrogant approach. He grabs her arm and drags her over to Mandla while his wild laugh chills her to the bone.

Matsisi is very pleased with himself. He intuitively knows that Danisile's scream was more than just a simple scream. He heard the pain hidden within its depth. When Mandla starts struggling with all his might against the hands holding him he knows he has found the weapon he was looking for.

"What have we here, pretty one?" he sneers. "Looks like my brother found himself a little amusement while I was gone. Not bad, not bad at all!" Unwanted passion suddenly wakes inside him at the sight of her wide delightful mouth and frightened eyes. He looks at her as if he wants to drink in everything he sees. Unable to resist he pulls her against him and kisses her passionately. When he lifts his head and sees the open disgust on her face, his passion leaves as quickly as it came. He grabs a handful of her hair and jerks her head back.

Mandla is beside himself and struggles with all his might against Matsisi's men. Their fingers bite harder into his flesh as they struggle to control him. "Let her go!" he screams at Matsisi, "It's me you want! Let her go!"

Matsisi grins and turns her so that her back is against his chest. Deliberately he puts his dirty hand on her firm, young breast. He cares little about the small desperate groan that escapes her. Slowly he takes the knife from his belt and pushes it against her throat.

Mandla shakes his head and screams at Matsisi. "No Matsisi! She's done nothing! It's me you want!"

Matsisi keeps the knife at Danisile throat. He looks at Mandla with hatred in his eyes. "You take from me and I take from you, an eye for an eye and a tooth for a tooth, hey brother." He shakes his head in feigned sadness. "It's a pity though, isn't it? She's such a pretty little thing," he says. He looks at Mandla for a while with dark and hard eyes then pulls his hand back and slits her throat in one quick movement.

Mandla and Danisile's eyes lock and they become frozen in time. This short frozen moment becomes the only moment they have. There is no past and there is no future, there is only now. Across the short, yet vast distance between them, their hearts, minds and souls are one.

Mandla screams hoarsely when blood gushes from the fatal cut and she falls to the ground with a soft groan. While her blood seeps into the ground she continues to look at him, but her eyes slowly lose their life and fade into nothingness. He is unaware of his desperate struggle against the imprisoning arms of Matsisi's men.

The elders are stunned and horrified and their hands fly up to cover their mouths. Some of the villagers, hiding behind the smooth and worn wooden poles on the outside perimeter of the meeting place, turn and run in fear. Tied to one of the benches Dumisai barks hysterically but no one seems to notice. Neither did anyone notice Thukani shuffle away with his cripple leg.

Everyone jerks with nervous fright when Matsisi stumbles forward and falls to the ground with a thud. Protruding from his back, like a pointing finger, is a spear. Numb with horror their eyes fly to the direction the spear came from. It is Thukani!

Thukani limps over to Matsisi. He pulls the spear from his son's back and blood gushes through the now open and gaping wound. Without help he rolls Matsisi on his back and kneels down beside him. His breathing is heavy and sweat pours down his face. It took everything he had to pull his arm back and throw the spear. He touches Matsisi's face tenderly with shaking fingers.

Matsisi's face is drained of all colours and his breath rasps in his throat. He is still alive, but barely. The sharp fierce pain in his back has subsided and all that he feels is his heart pounding in his chest. He looks up at Thukani with an unspoken question on his lips.

Thukani wipes his hand over his face and it leaves a streak of blood on his cheek. "I threw the spear my son," he says in a broken voice.

Matsisi looks at his father with wide eyes. It is almost as if can he cannot comprehend what his father is saying to him. He tries to sit up but can't. "Why?" he whispers to his father. "Why?"Tears blur Thukani's vision. He grabs Matsisi's hands tightly. He holds them as if he wants to keep the life force in his dying son a bit longer. "My son you are like a wounded buffalo. I have wounded you by not giving you the love you deserve, and you have taken revenge on me by wounding our people. It's time for the wounded buffalo to be at peace. I'm sorry my son.................there was no other way............"

Matsisi's eyes bore into his father's. His body shivers and shakes with the effort to breathe with his injured lung. Blood is seeping out of his mouth and his body gives up the last desperate effort. His head rolls to one side as the last life sustaining breath leaves his body. Dimly his father's words, about a wounded buffalo, echo through his mind. Is that what he was? He doesn't know.

Thukani drops Matsisi's lifeless hands just as the fish eagle sharp call pierces the silence again. He struggles to his feet. Bongwe rushes to help him but he shakes of his hand and gets up unaided. He turns to Matsisi's men and gives them a curt order to let Mandla go. They hesitate for only a small moment, and then obey. They have no bravado left now that their leader is dead. When Thukani orders with dark eyes. "Go! Leave now!" they turn and run.

Chapter 15
Nothing Remains the Same

Matsisi's men lets Mandla go and he runs over to Danisile. He kneels next to her and calls her name in a hoarse voice. He pulls her lifeless body towards him and cradles her against his chest. He rocks forward and backwards, if only he could use his own heartbeat to bring her back to life again. He strokes her blood-clotted hair and his fingers become stained with the last of her life force.

Thukani limps over to him, put his hand on his shoulder and say. "There is nothing you can do Mandla, she is gone," but Mandla ignores him and continues rocking Danisile.

With slow and tired movements some of the elders get up. With hunched shoulders they start shuffling home. Thukani is right, there's nothing more they can do.

Mandla lets Danisile go when Bongwe pulls her from his grip. He watches him cover her with a blanket. All that is left of the Danisile he knew is just a lifeless body. He groans and gets up. "Why?" he shouts at Bongwe and Thukani. "Why did she have to die?"

"I don't know why Danisile had to die." Thukani answers. "I only know why Matsisi had to die." He steps forward, takes Mandla by the shoulders and says. "Once I killed you so that your brother may live. Today I killed your brother so that you may live."

Mandla eyes widen with the horror of his father's words. He steps back and shakes Thukani's hands off his shoulders with disgust.

Without a word he turns around and runs out of the meeting place. There is no understanding in his heart or mind for anything that has happened today.

"Mandla!" Bongwe calls and turns to follow him.

Thukani grips his arm and holds him back. He shakes his head. "Let him be my friend, there are some battles one needs to fight alone." When Bongwe steps back he limps over to Dumisai and starts untying him. He walks away with a surprisingly docile Dumisai at his heels. He will take care of Matsisi's dog himself. His own sorrow he will keep deep inside him for now. Later he will mourn and make peace with what he did.

A still seated Sibongile watches Bongwe follow her father. She doesn't want to get up because she's not sure that her legs will carry her. She stays seated, staring into nowhere until the meeting place is empty. When the last elder shuffle out the entrance, she puts her head in her hands and cries. Not harsh and angry but soft and scared.

Eventually her soft sobs subside and she calms down. She wipes the tears from her face just as the fish eagle lets out another long dramatic call. She jerks her head up to look at him perched on the high branches of a nearby tree. He has a white head and breast, chestnut belly, black wings and a white tail. He throws back his head and gives another haunting cry and she can hear an answering call in the distance. He lifts off and flies to the nearby river where he will swoop down and pluck a fish from the water to give to his mate to feed their young.

Sibongile frowns. She heard the fish eagle call pierce the silence just as Danisile died and she heard it when Matsisi died as well. Could it mean anything? She shrugs her shoulders, maybe it does, and maybe it doesn't. Right now the hardest memory she would like to erase is a glinting spear flying through the air to find a deadly mark.

When the night birds begin a plaintive chorus she takes a deep breath, gets up and starts walking home. Nothing ever stays the same.

The Spirit People appear in the world of form, as they have done since the beginning of time. Their joyful dancing is absent as they set about doing what needs to be done.

They need to thank the fish eagle first. He was the one that spread his large wings, swooped down and lifted Danisile's spirit from her lifeless body. He did the same for Matsisi. In turn, he carried each of them on his wings to the Spirit People, so they can take care of them. For the Spirit People there is no real difference between Matsisi, Danisile or anyone else. The holiness everyone shares is never compromised.

Their movements are slow and sad, another peaceful solution failed because of fear. They glimmer in the moonlight to shake off the depressive feelings. They have work to do! All conditions are temporary.

Mandla's mouth is pulled in a bitter line and his breathing uneven and hard. He walks, runs, and doesn't even know or care where he is going. The long grass twirls around his ankles as if it wants to slow him down, and he trips and falls. He jerks it out of the way, gets up and looks straight into the eyes of a wild dog.

It is black-skinned, long-legged and covered with short, sparse fur in a wide range of black, yellow and white patterns. It twitches its large and round ears.

Mandla pulls up his shoulders in a no-care attitude, then turns and continues stomping through the bushes. He knows wild dogs travel in large packs and are well-organized, efficient hunters. Yet, at this very moment, he doesn't care.

He had only gone a short distance when the long grass ensnares his ankles once more and he crashes down again. He gets up slowly and wipes his now bruised and bloodied hand over his face. He shows no emotion, anger or otherwise, for losing his balance and falling. He is just about to walk away again when he sees a cave entrance in front of him. Without even thinking about it he walks inside.

He looks around the cave half-heartedly. Even though there is a stack of dry wood it is obvious no one has been here for a long time. Silvery spider webs weave intricate patterns covering large areas. Apart from that, it is as cold and empty as he is. Deathly tired he sits down on the cold and hard floor.

His thoughts dash to Danisile and he buries his face in his hands. Hot tears and angry sobs burst from inside him. It bubbles to the surface with a force that he is unable to control. His whole being immerses in a painful sorrow that can only be released through tears. When he eventually stops, all that is left is his anger, nothing more.

He rubs his arms when the cold of the cave seeps into him. With a shiver he gets up and uses the dry wood in the cave to build a fire.

His hands shake but a spiral of smoke indicates the beginning of a flame. Soon the flames are dancing and the fire spluttering but Mandla continues to throw more wood on the fire. Red-hot embers fly in all directions and the flames stretch and grow. When the flames nearly touch the roof of the cave, he stops and sits down dangerously close to the fire. The air in the cave has become thick and hot, but he doesn't care. The fire has become an outlet for his anger.

Sweat is pouring down his body from the intense heat. With some form of sense returning between his anger and bitterness, he gets up and moves away from the heat. With a big sigh he lays down knowing full well that sleep won't come easy tonight. His mind begins to follow a process of enquiry, but no matter how hard he tries, he cannot make sense of what has happened.

He suddenly sits upright and glares at the blazing fire with dark eyes. With a bitter voice he snarls. "The flame of life has burned my soul to ashes and nothing could stop it. Not even God, because God doesn't exist!"

He looks past the fire into the darkness of the cave that stretches beyond. It feels as cold and empty as he does, and it strengthens his conclusion that God doesn't exists. Everything is just a daily task of existence. Stress, strive and scenarios that come forth for no reason whatsoever, except to bring pain.

The Spirit People slide down the moonbeams to comfort Mandla. They touch him with feather light fingers and wish they could take his pain away, but they can't. They cannot undo what has been done.

In between the moonbeams that penetrated the entrance of the cave they surround him and lift their arms high. They open their hearts and send their own inner moonbeams to enter Mandla. In their own moonbeams they give their love, their compassion, their care and understanding.

When they hear Mandla's bitter snarl that God doesn't exist, they gasp in horror. They shiver and shake as if an ice cold wind had just swept through them. Quickly they withdraw their healing rays and cross their arms over their hearts. They will not give their love to someone who makes such an astonishing claim! They stare at the dismal-looking Mandla and shake their heads in disbelief. Surely everyone can see that the breath of God is in everything?

The Spirit People frown when a light wind, containing a powerful energy starts entering the cave. It increases and becomes a forceful gale that pushes them deeper into the darkness of the cave. A bright and crystalline light flash and the Spirit People cover their eyes with their feather light fingers. When it stops, they slowly take their hands away and look around frightened and confused. Then they see him. It is The One!

When he opens his arms and holds out his hands, they rush forward. He embraces them and they cling to the comfort of his presence like frightened children. Mandla's words had plunged them into a deep darkness.

"Do you believe God doesn't exist?" The One asks them in his gentle voice.

"No! No!" they answer indignantly.

"Then why did you withdraw your love?" He asks the Spirit People. "Do you perhaps consider it wrong to give love to someone who claims God doesn't exists?"

The Spirit People hang their heads in shame. They should have known better. When The One says with infinite tenderness, "One needs love the most when he deserves it the least," they feel a sharp pain in their hearts. A painful observation is always a truthful one. They have allowed what they shared with Mandla to be compromised.

The One steps forward and lifts his hands towards Mandla. The Spirit People doesn't hesitate. They join him and stretch their arms out as far as they can. From deep within their souls they gather all their energy. They use all the love they have, from the very depths of their beings, and send it to Mandla. Their combined energy multiplies and surrounds Mandla with its loving force.

"Sleep Beloved," they whisper to Mandla and help him into the nothingness that only sleep can bring. They will show him that there is never a time when he is alone. God is always with him.

Chapter 16

Feelings is the Language of the Soul

Mandla wakes up just as the sun shoots its bright rays into the cave. With a groan he struggles to get up. His body is bruised, stiff and sore and caked with dried blood. His clothes are dirty and dishevelled.

He looks at the left over embers of the dying fire. The whole cave feels oppressive as if the walls are pressing down on him. He turns and walks outside but has to hold his right hand over his ribs cage as it hurts with every breath that he takes. His left eye is purple and so swollen that he cannot even see through it.

With difficulty he makes his way to the river that he vaguely remembers passing yesterday. To his relief he finds it not far from the cave. He bends down to drink from the cool water, but has to wait for the pain in his ribs to subside before he can do so. Once he had quenched his thirst he tries to clean himself but it is too painful. Exhausted from the effort he struggles back to the cave.

At the entrance of the cave he sags down on a big rock. His breathing is painful, uneven and difficult. After sitting outside the cave for a while he feels better but cannot bring himself to enter. It is almost as if the cave represents his open and festering wound and he's reluctant to face it again. He feels for a moment he's glad to be alone, but a painful stab reminds him that it isn't really what he wants.

The sun's rays bounce off him in the crisp morning air and he resents its seeming happiness. "What have you got to be so happy about?" he grunts. "Not that you have anything to be unhappy about either, now do you?" he continues. "You get up in the morning and go to sleep at night, no worries, no pain, not a care in the world. You don't care if there is a God or what God does or doesn't do."

He squints his one functioning eye and glares at the sun. "I wonder if you can think about something. Can you? Can you think about something and find the answer? He shrugs his shoulders. "If you can, you're better than I am because I can't find any answers by thinking about it." He feels lightheaded and with a grunt gets up and walks into the cave while mumbling. "If I don't find answers soon I'll probably go out of my mind."

Inside the cave Mandla lowers himself very slowly and lies down. Even though it is still early morning, he is deathly tired from the effort of walking to the river. On top of that, the vicious cycle of negative and bitter thoughts are quickly returning. With a deep sigh he closes his eyes. It doesn't take long for him to get pulled into the darkness of sleep in the land of nothingness.

The land of nothingness is also the entrance to the dream world. Sometimes dreams are good and sometimes not so good, but they will be received, by the willing as well as the unwilling.

When the beginning clouds of the dream world clear, Mandla finds himself standing underneath a jacaranda tree. It is filled with clusters of fragrant purple, trumpet-shaped blooms. There is a river and on its banks a large waterbuck is grazing. He has a coarse, saggy coat that is reddish-brown in colour. His ringed horns are long and curved and on his rump is a white elliptical ring. Mandla starts walking towards the waterbuck but swings around when he hears Danisile's infectious laughter behind him.

With a bouncing heart he runs in the direction of the sound but cannot find her. He runs back when he hears her laughing behind the jacaranda tree but when he gets there, she is not there either. He scans the area and strains his ears for any sign of her, but there is nothing. Miserable and depressed he sags down underneath the tree and puts his head in his hands.

He is jerked out of his misery when her delightful giggle jingles in front of him. He looks up and she is standing in front of him. She looks beautiful! She is dressed in a long white robe and her face is peaceful and happy.

Mandla jumps up and embraces her. He buries his face in her hair and smells her sweet scent. "I'll never let you go again," he groans. "Never!"

Danisile disentangles herself from his embrace and steps back. She shakes her head and her big brown eyes look almost sad. "I can't stay Mandla," she says, "I have to go back."

"No!" he shouts. "If it's about Matsisi hurting you I'm sorry! I tried to stop him but I couldn't! I'm sorry I couldn't protect you!" He takes a deep breath to calm himself. "Please don't leave me again," he pleads while his guilt hangs like a heavy cloak around him, "I don't think I can bear it."

Danisile shakes her head. "Stop feeling guilty about what happened my love, it's not your fault."

"Then you will stay?" he says with a joyful tilt in his voice and steps forward to embrace her again.

She stops him and shakes her head. "No Mandla I can't stay. I have to go back."

"Back where?" he asks in a tight voice. "Why can't you stay?"

"I have to go back to the Spirit World," she says tenderly.

"So God has taken you from me! Why would He do that?" Mandla grinds through clenched teeth.

Danisile takes his hand. "No Mandla, God didn't take me away from you. I am still very much alive, all that I left behind is my body."

"Then I will join you in the Spirit World," Mandla says and touches her hair with shaking fingers. "I don't want to continue living without you, it is too painful."

She gives a soft laugh. "No Mandla. Don't take the power of life and death in your hands. It is more important that you share what you have learned. The world needs it."

"What did I learn that is so important to share?" he asks despondently.

"People need to learn loving each other without wants and needs. They need to learn to stop trying to change each other, and allow each other the freedom to express themselves."

"How do you expect me to teach them that?" he asks in disbelief.

"You don't have to teach them," she says. "Show them by example. You allowed me to experience who and what I am through our love. You can do the same for others." She steps back, turns and slowly starts walking away.

Mandla tries to follow her but can't move. His feet are rooted to the ground. She stops and turns around. "The only thing you can take with you into the next life is love," he hears he say before she disappears in a hazy mist that now surrounds her.

Mandla stirs and groans when the dream world lets him go. He returns to the darkness and nothingness of sleep but her sweet scent lingers around him.

In the dark shadows of the cave the Spirit People keep watch. They guided him into the dream world and will make sure of his save return to the world of form.

Not far from the cave Sibongile is making her way through the bushes. She has been out of her mind worrying about Mandla and decided to go and look for him. Always prepared, as usual, she carries a bag containing food and water. Her steps quicken when she sees the tell tale signs where Mandla stomped through the bushes. Grasses are pressed down and splatters of dried blood and torn clothing cling like lifelines on the tips of thin branches. She follows his obvious trail easily, yet knowing in her heart that she is being guided to him.

She is so focused on following Mandla that she jumps with fright when a young man steps out in front of her. Her hand flies to her heart to stop it jumping out of her chest and she takes a deep breath to give the loudest scream of her life.

The young man holds up his hands indicating that he means her no harm. "Don't be afraid," he says in a deep voice. "I'm not going to harm you."

Tense and tight Sibongile takes a step back. Her eyes are large in her face and her mouth pulled tight. Meeting a stranger in the bushes can lead to anything. "What do you want?" she says in a high voice.

The young man's eyes sparkle, he gives her a small bow and says. "My name is Sizwe and I sincerely apologize for giving you such a big fright."

Sibongile hears the compliment but it does nothing to reassure her. She doesn't know him, therefore doesn't trust him, it is as simple as that. She looks him up and down, pushes her chin out and says with defiance. "I am Sibongile, the oldest daughter of Thukani."

"Mmmmmmmm...." Sizwe says rubbing his chin. "I have heard of Thukani. He is the territorial chief, isn't he?" He walks over to Sibongile and lightly runs his index finger down her high cheekbone. "No one told me he had such a pretty daughter though."

Sibongile slaps his hand away and says with flashing eyes. "Don't you dare touch me!"

He laughs in his deep voice and steps back holding up his hands again. What a stroke of luck bumping into the lovely Sibongile, dressed all neat and tidy with matching dress and head cloth, and big brown eyes you can drown in.

Sibongile watches him wearily but can't help noticing that his wide attractive smile flashes white and perfect teeth. His chest is broad, bulging with muscles, and his head is clean-shaven. Around his waist he wears a soft impala skin.

"Let's start over again." Sizwe says with a small humorous smile. "I'm sorry for touching you, I just couldn't resist your beauty." She blushes at his compliment and it makes him like her even more. A crested barbet lets out a long, sustained trilling "Trrrrrr" above him and it reminds him that he has a mission to complete. He immediately becomes serious. "I am looking for a man called Mandla. Do you know him or have you heard of him?"

"What do you want with Mandla?" Sibongile asks defensively but with cheeks still a bit flushed.

"So you know him?" Sizwe says. "What a relief. I need to find him a soon as I can because Mthisa is very ill." He shakes his head sadly. "There's not much time left."

"Mthisa?" The woman that raised him?" Sibongile asks.

Sizwe nods his head. "Do you know where I can find Mandla?"

"Not really." Sibongile says. "I'm also trying to find him." Sizwe looks at her so intently that she feels like he is reading her mind. Embarrassed she looks down at the trail marks she had been following.

"Mmmmmmmm..........." he says in his deep voice following her gaze. "Then we will just have to find him together, won't we?" He looks down at the squashed grass and red tipped branches. "Mmmmmmm........." He looks around a bit more then gestures to her to follow him. "Come, he went this way."

Sibongile follows him without a word. She is thankful that he is silent but also that he seems to know exactly how to track and find Mandla. It's not long before they come to the entrance of the cave. Sizwe starts going inside but she hangs back. She hates the darkness of caves.

When he notices her hesitation to enter, he takes her hand in a firm grip and leads her inside while saying in a reassurance voice. "Don't be afraid. Everything will be alright."

In the dim light she sees Mandla on the cave floor. With a small scream she rushes over to him. "Mandla!" she croaks in a hoarse voice and touches his shoulder. "Mandla! Are you alright?"

Mandla groans and opens his eyes. "Danisile!" he mumbles.

Sizwe bends down next to Sibongile and looks at Mandla's unfocussed gaze, but not before he had seen the pain flash in Sibongile's eyes. He pretends he didn't notice and says. "He is in a deep sleep, a good time to tend to his wounds."

By the time the sun started dropping behind the horizon Sibongile had finished cleaning the unconscious Mandla and tending to his wounds. Sizwe collected dry wood and made a fire and she prepared some of the food she carried with her in her bag. She didn't eat much but Sizwe certainly made a meal of it. A bit of an uncomfortable silence settles around them.

She jumps with fright when Sizwe asks her. "Are you in love with him?" She answers indignantly, "Of course not! He is my half-brother!" When his response is a nod of his head and his usual,

"Mmmmmmmmmm…………." it irritates her immensely. "Stop pretending that you know everything!" she snaps at him.

He stares at the smouldering coals of the fire and says in his deep voice. "You know Sibongile you can never escape your own mind. You can go to the highest mountain and still find your thoughts there. Even if you bury yourself underground your thoughts will still be there." He looks over to the sleeping Mandla. "Like Mandla you could try and hide in a cave but your thoughts will follow. There is nowhere you can go to escape your own mind. Your thoughts will always be there."

"So what!" Sibongile says and shrugs her shoulders. "I'm not trying to stop my thoughts."

"Yes you are," Sizwe says with an intent look in his ever-sparkling eyes. "You are also trying to find answers by thinking about it, but the mind can never find anything. The only way to find the answers you seek is through the path of your heart."

Sibongile stares at Sizwe with new eyes. "I don't understand," she says softly.

He gives her a gentle smile. "Feelings are the language of the soul. Stop thinking about things and get back to your senses, in other words how you feel about it. When you do this, you are in a state of equal balance and the truth will come. Instead of thinking about a problem, just be with it, and you will find the answers you are looking for."

He lifts his hand and runs his finger down the soft smooth skin of her high cheekbone and Sibongile swallows hard at the effect it has on her. He leans closer and his breath tickles her face when he says. "Sibongile get out of your mind and simply be." Her hand is still fluttering to her thumping heart when he gets up and walks out of the cave.

Sibongile stares at the flames licking like hungry predators at the dry wood. She jumps up when Mandla stirs and runs to his side. She calls his name softly but he remains unresponsive. Tentatively she puts her hand on his chest but withdraws it quickly when he stirs again. She gives a big sigh, gets up and returns to her seat next to the fire. Her thoughts are in more turmoil than what she would ever believe possible. When Sizwe eventually returns she jumps up and literally runs out of the cave.

Outside the cave Sibongile sits down on a big rock, unknown to her, the same one Mandla was sitting on before. It is as if the rock was specially placed there for someone who wants to sit and think. She looks up at the moon. It is bright and beautiful tonight. She closes her eyes and lifts her face to the moon. It feels like the moonbeams are touching her skin and she lets out a slow content breath. Thoughts jumps into her mind and she stills them. All she wants right now is the peace and tranquillity the moon always seems to give her. A small smile plays on her lips, for now she is free of the crashing waves of her thoughts.

Her eyes fly open when a feeling so strong and potent, that she couldn't stop it, flashes through her. She's not in love with Mandla! No! She's in love with the idea of being in love! She wanted so badly to have someone hold her tight under the moonlight and whisper sweet love words to her, that she imagined that person to be Mandla. She shakes her head. How could she, Sibongile, who has always been the logical and practical one, have allowed herself to be so silly? Is she so desperate for someone to love that she has to create a scenario in her mind?

She squeezes her eyes closed when hot tears start running down her cheeks. She doesn't get a fright when Sizwe sits down next to her and puts his arm across her shoulders. She doesn't even object when he drops a light kiss on her head. It just feels right.

The Spirit People giggle in the moonlight. They look at the moon and it becomes brighter, while lazily blinking its huge bright eyes. Its voice is slow and steady, like the age old being that it is. "Only when humans start listening to the universal language of the soul can they live in the same tranquillity as nature."

The Spirit People start dancing. They jump from moonbeam to moonbeam. Something sweet is in the air tonight and it is a distinct possibility that it is Sibongile and Sizwe.

Chapter 17
Love, the Greatest Gift of All

Mandla wakes up with a start. He sits up slowly and puts his hands on both sides of his head. His head is pounding like he has had too much corn beer. Bright sunlight pours into the cave making it appear to be a much happier place. A small fire hisses and crackles not far from him, and next to it, a bowl of food.

With difficulty he gets up and sees that someone has tended to his wounds and cleaned him up. His stomach groans and he shuffles over to the food. Without concerning himself who left it there, he picks it up and starts eating. He only has a small amount of food before he feels full and puts the bowl down. Slowly he sits down again. He feels as if his legs won't be able to carry him for long. He looks up when he hears voices and Sibongile and Sizwe walk into the cave.

Sibongile drops the dry wood she is carrying and runs over to him. "Mandla! Are you all right? How are you feeling?" She asks with concern all over her voice and manner.

He shrugs his shoulders not bothering to reply. He looks over to Sizwe. "Who are you?" he asks looking him up and down.

Sizwe doesn't answer the rude question. He walks into the cave and drops his load of dry wood. He turns to Sibongile. "Mandla has enough food and firewood to keep him going till he gets well. We can return to the village."

But…. but…who is going to take care of him?" a surprised Sibongile stutters. "I'm sure he'll manage." Sizwe says and starts gathering their things.

Mandla gives a snort through his nose and ignores them both. He simply doesn't care.

Sibongile touches Mandla's shoulder, "Mandla?" she asks concerned.

He shakes off her hand and snaps. "Just go! I want to be alone!"

Without another word Sibongile lifts her head, spins around and walks over to the already waiting Sizwe. She starts walking out, but stops and starts turning back to talk to Mandla again. Sizwe takes her hand and pulls her along with him. "Wait!" she resists, "We just can't leave him alone! Who's going to take care of him?"

"He'll be fine." Sizwe says calmly.

"What about the message you have to give him? What about Mthisa?" Sibongile insists.

Sizwe stops but keeps hold of her hand. "Right now Mandla needs to be alone."

"Why?" a confused Sibongile asks. "He still needs my help."

"There are things that needs to happen to Mandla before he'll understand fully the path he's on," he says.

"What kind of things?" Sibongile wants to know.

He gives a deep sigh. He can see she won't leave till he explains more. "Mandla didn't stumble upon this cave by accident, he was drawn here. It is Mthisa's cave. It is here in this cave, where his journey began and from here he will continue to the next stage of his

186

journey. He cannot do so when we are with him. Some roads need to be followed alone."

"How do you know this?" Sibongile asks.

"We have a mutual friend called Tanua." Sizwe says and starts walking again. "Let's go. If we stay here any longer I might have to kiss your pretty mouth."

Sibongile is unable to stop a giggle bubbling to the top. "Mmmmmmmm," she hears Sizwe say and this time it sounds like music to her ears.

Inside the cave Mandla hears their voices fade into the distance. His mood is even more morose now. Clouds have moved in front of the sun and the cave doesn't look so happy and bright anymore. Not that it makes any difference, he feels as if all life has been withdrawn from him anyway. He gets up and walks out of the cave, mumbling under his breath and holding his hand over his bruised ribs. He just walks into a nowhere direction. Nothing makes sense anymore.

He gives a snort and spits on the ground. "My whole life is just one misery after another." He looks up at the sky and calls. "Hey Tanua, all those gift given to me by your so called God means nothing because God doesn't exist!"

A playful wind tucks at his long hair and blows sand into his eyes. Irritated he rubs his eyes but jerks his head up when he hears a deep groaning whisper. "God exists and He is here." He looks around half-heartedly and the deep voice whispers again. "God exists and He is here. When his birthmark starts burning it increases his irritation. "Who are you? Who's talking?" he snaps with a frown.

"It is I, everything that is," the deep voice groans and at the same time the wind becomes stronger.

Mandla looks around trying to locate the speaker and his frown deepens when he realizes that he is in what seems to be a forest of yellow wood trees. The trees are very tall with thick trunks and broad, dense crowns. He shakes his head, he can't remember seeing all the trees before. The wind now gushes through the trees and the treetops begin to sway from side to side. They crack and groan and pieces of dry bark shower down on Mandla. Other voices join the deep moaning and the growing chorus feels like it is exploding in his head. He puts his hand over his ears and shouts. "Stop it!"

The yellow wood trees continue to sway and groan. They lean from side to side in unison and move to the beat of a sound that only they can hear. Mandla shouts at them to stop again, but his voice is small and insignificant against the deep groans. All he can do against the defeating noise is press his hands over his ears as hard as he can.

Suddenly the noise stops and the trees stand still and solid again. With relief Mandla slowly takes his hands away from his ears. The silence that now greets him is almost as great as the deafening noise that preceded it. When the burning, stinging sensation in his birthmark increases he deliberately ignores it. All he wants is to get as far away from this place as he can.

He grinds his teeth in frustration when he realizes the trees have closed around him like a triangle. The trunks are so close together that he can't even squeeze through. "What are you doing?" he shouts.

"I am not interested in speaking to Tanua or anyone else. All I want is to be alone! Is that so hard to understand?"

Full of anger he kicks at a bush in front of him and dry leaves scatter in the air. He hobbles over to the nearest tree and start beating the tree trunk with his fists. Out of breath, he soon has to stop his useless effort. Emotionally drained he sags down. His chest burns with the same intensity as his birthmark. He puts his head and his hands and mumbles. "Nothing anyone can say will make a difference. Nothing can take away the pain of yesterday, the pain of today, or the pain of tomorrow." He slowly lifts his head and looks at the towering treetops. "You may have trapped by body, but my mind is still my own!" he shouts and closes his eyes.

Above the treetops the sun continues its slow steady movement through the sky. Mandla wipes the sweat from his forehead with the back of his hand. It is hot and stuffy between the trees. He has been trapped for hours and nothing has happened. He struggles to get up while holding on to his injured ribcage. His irritation boils to the surface and he looks up the sky and shouts. "Tanua! Where are you?" but only silence answers back. He bangs his fist into a tree again and shouts. "How long do you want me to just sit here and wait? Is it your intention to keep me trapped here till I'm also dead? Do you want me to join Danisile and Matsisi? Do you want me to stay here till the rodents and buzzards have picked my body clean? Is that what you want?"

A tree, larger than all the others, begins to glow. A bright beam emerges from the tree and begins to stretch itself lazily towards the sky. Beautiful soft colours begin to form on the light-beam and it looks like blue-green, pink, yellow and violet crystals catching a ride on a rainbow.

Mandla's birthmark stings even more and a pulling sensation in the centre of his forehead become so strong that it feels like a blinding headache. The beam of light from the tree stretches higher and higher into the sky till Mandla cannot even see the end. It makes a strange humming noise as if it is alive and vibrating with energy.

With amazement Mandla sees that a man is easily walking down the beam. He shakes his head in disbelief. How is it possible that a man can walk on a beam of light? When the man gets to the ground he steps off the beam and it dissipates into the air. It leaves in its wake, shiny specks of silver and gold. A gust of wind appears, scoops up the shiny specks, forms a spiral and whirls them away.

The man now standing in front of Mandla is tall and slender. He is dressed in a long white robe that hangs loosely on his body. He has brown curly hair that touches his shoulders and a small smile on his wide mouth. His eyes are his most stunning feature, they are deep blue and sparkle and shine like two brilliant stars.

Mandla feels quite in awe. The man seems to radiate an enormous amount of powerful energy. He asks in a low voice. "Who are you? What do you want?"

"I am Jeshua," is the soft response. "I want nothing from you. I came to give you a message from God."

Anger and bitterness immediately busts from Mandla's body and soul. With a dark frown he says in a loud voice. "No! I don't believe you! I'm sick and tired of hearing God sent me, or God said this or that. If He really wants to give me messages and gifts, why doesn't He come here himself? I'll tell you why! Because He can't! He doesn't exist!"

Jeshua seems unperturbed at Mandla's outburst. "Why would you think something like that?" he asks.

"Because if God existed, He wouldn't have allowed all those horrible things to happen in my life!" Mandla raves on.

"Was it God's hand that held the knife that killed Danisile or the spear that killed Matsisi?" Jeshua asks. "Or do you think that it was God's intension to let bad things to happen to you?"

"Obviously!" Mandla says sarcastically.

Jeshua steps forward, puts his hand on Mandla's shoulder and says. "If you are prepared to accept you are being treated, whether it is good or bad by God, you are in fact admitting that God does exists."

Tense and tight Mandla clenches his fist. He doesn't want to have this conversation. He feels trapped and claustrophobic. All he wants is for things to be the way they were.

Jeshua takes Mandla's arm and leads him towards a fallen tree trunk with gentle, yet firm hands. He sits down and without wanting to, Mandla sits down beside him.

"God doesn't want you to suffer Mandla," Jeshua says. "In fact, nothing would give Him greater pleasure than to see each and every person living a happy and fulfilling life. It is well within His power to change anything He wants, yet He cannot do so without breaking His promise to you."

Mandla jerks his head up. "What promise?"

"The promise of a free will." Jeshua says." You see Mandla you were born so that you could experience life on earth any way you wish. Sometimes these experiences will unpleasant and sometimes they will be pleasant. Yet every experience you have is perfect for you. That is why every experience in your life, is a blessing."

Mandla jumps up and glares at Jeshua. "How can you expect me to see what happened as a blessing?" he grins through his teeth. "I tried to stop the people killing my brother and ended up losing Danisile. How can that be a blessing?" He walks away only to turn back again. "Now you are trying to tell me that it was a perfect experience? If it was such a perfect experience I would have been able to change the way things happened and things wouldn't have gone so horribly wrong."

Jeshua answers in his soft voice. "If an experience is unpleasant it doesn't mean it's wrong. It only means your concept of it makes it appear wrong or horrible. Right now all you feel is the pain of the experience, but it was still a perfect experience for you. Once you can understand this, every experience you have, becomes a blessing and not a curse."

Mandla shakes his head. "I don't know if I can ever see what happened as a blessing."

"You will Beloved," Jeshua says, "when you accept that God is life and life is change."

"Beloved? You've just called me Beloved? Mandla says with raised eyebrows. Why would you call me that?" When Jeshua looks up at him with his brilliant penetrating eyes he feels as if Jeshua is looking deep within his soul.

"God calls everyone Beloved." Jeshua says tenderly.

A shiver runs down Mandla's spine. He swallows hard and stutters. "Are... are you God?"

Jeshua gives a small smile. "No I'm not God, thought I am part of God, just as you are part of God."

Mandla shakes his head and gives a sad smile. "I don't deserve to be called Beloved by you or anyone else. I tried to change the world and failed."

Jeshua gets up, walks over to Mandla and gives his shoulder a comforting squeeze. "Beloved just because not everyone heard what you said, doesn't mean that one stops trying. Sometimes people will treat you with contempt and sometimes they will even mock you, but hold on to your intentions. Show them by example instead of trying to change them with words. Remember what you do, is always a reflection of what your life is about. If you hold on to your intensions God will give you the necessary tools you need to change not only yourself, but also everyone around you."

Mandla stares at Jeshua and swallows hard. He doesn't know what to say.

Jeshua continues. "You have been given the gift of Courage, Patience and Understanding. Now I am giving you the gift of Clarity. Know with clarity that there is only one thing in the world, and that is love. God only knows one thing and that is love. When you know only love, you will understand that there is no such thing as good or bad people in the world. You will start giving the gifts you have received to others and the circle will be complete."

Jeshua takes Mandla's arm and leads him back to the fallen tree trunk. Mandla sits down and takes a deep breath. For the first time since the nightmare began he feels calm, and the anger and bitterness stops swirling in his head.

Out of nowhere a wooden container filled with clear sparkling water appears. Jeshua bends down in front of Mandla, takes of his leather sandals and tenderly starts washing his feet.

Mandla has a lump in his throat. He opens his mouth to speak but cannot. He has never experienced such humility or love. Tears start running down his cheeks and he wipes them away with the back of his hand. Only now he knows what it means not to merely speak of love, but to live it every moment.

When Jeshua finished washing Mandla's feet, he gets up and looks at him with deep tender love in his brilliant deep blue eyes. A soft wind lifts his brown curls and flutters around his feet. The leaves in the tree above them rustle and it sounds like a thousand tinkering bells cascading down on them. In his soft and gentle voice Jeshua says:

"Beloved, though I speak with the tongues of men and angels, and have not love, I will be like sounding brass or a tinkering cymbal.

And though I have the gift of prophecy, and understand all mysteries, and all knowledge; and though I have all faith, so that I could move mountains, and have not love, I am nothing.

And though I bestow all my goods to feed the poor, and though I give my body to be burned, and have not love, I gain nothing.

Love is patient and kind, love doesn't envy, love doesn't boast, and love isn't arrogant or rude. Love doesn't behave itself unseemly, love doesn't seek her own way and love is not easily provoked. Love rejoices not in iniquity, but rejoices in the truth.

Love bears all things, believes all things, embraces all things, and endures all things. Love is eternal. It never ends.

Whether there are prophecies, they shall fail. Whether there are tongues, they shall cease. Whether there is knowledge, it shall vanish away. For you think of yourself as a separate part of love. But once you act as a perfect part of love, then the separate part will fall away.

When I was a child, I spoke as a child, I understood as a child, I thought as a child; but when I discovered love, I put childish things away. Then I saw through a glass, darkly; but now clearly face to face. For I know now, I am not separate from love but a part thereof.

Now you can fully understand just as I fully understand, and as you are fully understood. And you will be known just as I am known.

Now abide in faith, hope, love, these three, but the greatest of these is love."

Mandla covers his eyes when there is a blinding flash. When he takes his hands away Jeshua is gone. He gets up and realises with

195

surprise that his ribs don't hurt anymore. He starts walking back to the cave. His path is clear and open. Everything is as it was.

When he reaches the cave he sits down on the rock outside. The sun is disappearing behind the horizon and the moon is slowly rising. They merge their energy as they always do when they meet. They splash the sky in a silky, pink, purple and blue. They are the creators of day and night. One cannot exist without the other.

Mandla sucks in his breath at the beauty and whispers to himself. "I have found God at last. He is in every breath that I take."

Chapter 18
It's not about Saying Something it's about Being Something

The Spirit People squeal with delight as they dance on the moonbeams. How exciting! Mandla met The One at last! They chatter in excited voices. Meeting Jeshua is always a life changing experience!

The age-old trees begin to groan and creek and without hesitation the Spirit People jump in between the quivering leaves. The trees are unsure, they don't think that Mandla understood that they were trying to share their own perfection with him. Under normal circumstances, they reveal little emotion when humans demonstrate their usual irrationality. They even seemed oblivious when he beat their trunks with his fists, but their roots, extended deep within the earth, quivered with pain.

The Spirit People jump down and embrace the tree trunks. They have come to understand that humans live on earth in a state of forgetfulness. They have forgotten how to find God, yet God has never been gone. He is always here and if you look for Him you'll always find Him. God is wherever you allow Him to be. They stroke the tree trunks with their feather light fingers. Trees give so much to humans yet get so little in return.

The trees become still and silent once more. They will continue to express the highest thought of who and what they are. Patiently they will wait for humans to discover the truth, no matter how long it takes.

The Spirit People start swirling and twirling between the trees. They are dancing the dance of life and they are not concerned about time. What is time anyway? They have all the time in the world!

Mandla wakes up in Mthisa's cave with bright sunlight warming his face. He gets up and starts preparing a meal with the last of the food left by Sibongile. After his meal he heads down to the river to wash. When he returns to the cave he intuitively knows it is time to leave. There is no need to stay here any longer.

He slowly looks around the cave. There is nothing here that he needs to take with him. For a moment anger and bitterness shoot through him like a knife stab. "I'll never come back here again," he says, "the memories are too painful." He swings around and walks out of the cave without looking back.

Surefooted he heads in the direction of the village. In the trees above him birds chirp and whistle. A secretary bird wearily watches him pass. It is bluish grey with very long legs, a long tail and hooked beak. It has a beautiful crest of long feathers, like a group of quill pens, behind his ear. As soon as he can't see Mandla anymore he continues to scan the area for snakes.

It is around midday when Mandla enters the village. People stop and stare at him, but he ignores them. It is a scorching hot day and all he wants is the cooling respite of Thukani's old Jacaranda tree.

Thukani and Bongwe had just settled down for their meal when they see him. With a wide smile Bongwe jumps up and runs forward to greet him. He can hardly hold in his excitement and chatter around him asking question upon question. He calls to the women to bring food and shoves a calabash filled with cornmeal beer into his hands. His high-excited voice causes gossipy women to peek out of their doorways.

When Mandla puts down the calabash and holds up his hands Bongwe grins with embarrassment. He sits down on the edge of his seat but rubs his puffy hands in anticipation.

Thukani acknowledges Mandla's greeting with a nod of his head. Inwardly he breathes a sigh of relief that Mandla has returned.

Bongwe tries to contain himself but can't. He blurts out. "Where have you been Mandla? Are you all right? What happened to your hair?"

Mandla takes a deep drink from the cool and refreshing cornmeal beer. He wipes his mouth with the back of his hand. "I am fine," he answers Bongwe "and nothing happened to my hair," he says a bit perplexed and touches it.

Bongwe leans forward and says in a low voice. "Your hair has a white streak in it!"

Mandla frowns and touches his long hair again. He shrugs his shoulders and shakes his head. "Don't know," he says and takes another drink of the cornmeal beer.

Thukani's eyes don't leave Mandla for a moment. He feels as if he wants to absorb everything he can from his son. He needs to ask Mandla if he'll be staying, but it is important that he waits for the right moment, he reasons in his mind. When is the right moment? He pulls his shoulders back and the question jumps out of his mouth. "Will you be staying?"

Mandla is not surprised by the question. In fact he has been expecting it. He puts down his cornmeal beer and shakes his head. "No, I am not staying."

Thukani jumps up and stumbles, forgetting for a moment his crippled leg. He holds on to the tree trunk for support and glares at Mandla. His mouth is tense and tight.

Mandla slowly gets up. With an unwavering gaze and firm, yet somehow gentle, voice he says to Thukani. "I cannot be what you want me to be. Even if I stayed and tried to be your successor, it will never work. It is not who I am."

Thukani's eyes give a dark flash and his mind races into ways he can force Mandla to obey him. He feels Bongwe place a calm hand on his shoulder and shakes it off with irritation. His legs feel as if they don't want to keep him upright anymore and he sits down. He closes his eyes to find some form of calmness in the darkness. A tingling sensation is pulsating through his body and with desperation he realizes he is repeating past mistakes. He takes a shuddering deep breath. Truth is always so uncomfortable. When he opens his eyes again he is calm, and the angry outburst that threatened to explode a moment ago, changes to a prolonged desperation.

"I will help you Mandla," he says in a low voice, "I will allow you all the freedom you need, just as I did Matsisi. You are so much more worthy than your brother to occupy the position of headsman. The people in the village need you."

Mandla gives a soft smile. "All of us are worthy father, one no more than the other. The differences in our lives are the choices we make. Yet, if we make a choice that is wrong it does not make us less worthy. We are all worthy, all of the time."

"But don't you hate Matsisi for what he did?" Bongwe bursts out with raised eyebrows.

Mandla shakes his head and looks down. "Hate is such a harsh word." He lifts his head and looks at Bongwe. "Let's just say my wounds have started healing."

"So you've forgiven Matsisi for his mistake?" Bongwe wants to know.

"There is no such thing as a mistake in the world and nothing happen by chance," Mandla answers and Bongwe frowns in confusion.

Sibongile enters and gives squeal of delight when she sees Mandla.

He gets up and embraces her. "Thank you for taking care of me," he whispers in her ear. He steps back to look at her and lifts his eyebrows. "You have a new light shining in your eyes. I wonder what it could be?"

Sibongile touches the head cloth matching her dress and turns to refill their empty calabashes. It also serves to hide the blush pushing up into her cheeks. "I will prepare a place for you to stay," she says with a bowed head.

"He's not staying." Bongwe says in a flat voice.

"Where are you going?" she asks, feeling a bit surprised at her own reaction. She thought she would be devastated if he leaves, but it doesn't seem to be so important anymore.

"I don't really know," Mandla answers honestly. "I intend to visit Mthisa for a while and then The Great Spirit will show me where to go from there. He will guide me. That is all I can really say about my plans, because it's all there is to my plans."

"How will the Great Spirit show you where to go Mandla? Do you talk to him?" Bongwe splutters in disbelief.

"Yes I do, Bongwe I talk to Him all the time." Mandla says.

"People will treat you with contempt if you say something like that! They'll think you're mad!" Bongwe says anxiously.

"No Bongwe, you don't understand. It's not about saying something. It is about being something. I want to share with everyone the wisdom I have learned. I want to show everyone I meet that no one is separate and individual. I want to show them that everyone and everything is the same. Once they see that every living thing is a part of the Great Spirit they will realize that He loves each and every one unconditionally. I want to share my knowledge so that they can understand as I have understood."

Thukani looks into the clear and direct eyes of his son. He is frustrated that he cannot penetrate the aura of strength Mandla seems to have around him. He looks away and gives a snort. "What about your responsibility?" he grunts.

"Father is right!" Sibongile pipes up. "You are his only heir, surely it is your responsibility to take over from him. He is your father!"

"No." Mandla says. "My only responsibility is to share the love I have with others. I have realized that love is all there is. Therefore everyone I meet is my brother and sister, and my mother and father."

Tense and tight Thukani struggles to his feet again. "Who will take over from me when I can no longer rule my people?" he snaps.

Mandla grins. "Your eldest daughter."

"But… but she…she's a woman!" Thukani stutters.

"It makes no difference." Mandla says. "All people are equal in the eyes of the Great Spirit. There is no difference between you, me or anyone else. We are all the same."

Sibongile looks at everyone with wide eyes. Such a thing has never even occurred to her. Besides not only is it against tradition, her father would never allow a woman to take over from him!

Bongwe walks over to Mandla and takes him by the shoulders. He wishes he could keep him there with invisible chains. "You can spread this love you talk about here," he implores him.

"It is not only up to me," Mandla says. "The Great Spirit has placed love in the heart of every person that is born. If everyone shared that love instead of just speaking about it, they will begin to live a life of love. No one will use violence to stop violence or anger to stop anger."

Desperately Bongwe tries again." We will need your help, or guidance, or at least your advice. How can we get it if you're not here."

"When you call, you will be answered, and when you ask, you will receive. Trust your feelings because that is one of the ways the Great Spirit talks to you." Mandla answers.

He embraces Bongwe, Sibongile and an unresponsive Thukani. With a small smile he turns around and walks away.

"Till we meet again my friend." Bongwe says hoarsely and turns his head to hide the uncontrollable tears filling his small eyes.

Sibongile watches Mandla till she can't see him anymore. She starts collecting the calabashes. Mandla and Sizwe are the same. They don't speak with the wisdom of the world. They speak with the wisdom of the Great Spirit.

On top of the hilltop Mandla stops and turns around to look at the village nestled below. The brightly painted huts decorate the countryside with beautiful colours. He doesn't know that he is standing in exactly the same spot Thukani stood while he waited for the elders to gather for a meeting to determine his fate. Not that it would have mattered had he known. He cannot change the past, only the future.

Not far from Mandla a kudu shakes its head with its long, spiralling magnificent horns. He is reddish-brown with a white stripe along the middle of his back and several white stripes on each side.

When Mandla turns to leave he notices the kudu but continues walking. The kudu won't attack him. They are timid and gentle animals. He doesn't notice anything else. His thoughts are with Mthisa.

Chapter 19

Every Person comes to you with a Gift in their Hands

It is still early morning when Thukani heads in the direction of the river. He wants to be alone so he can think. Now that he doesn't hide in the darkness of his mind anymore, he finds it hard to think with the hustle and bustle of daily life around him.

A warthog dashes in front of him and he stumbles and swears under his breath. The warthog has a stocky body with thin legs and a long furry tail. On his long, wide head there are two tusks and two pairs of wart-like protuberances. He gives a big sigh of relief when it disappears into the bushes, the warthog's tusks can be used as a deadly weapon.

He continues to limp further into the bushes but after a while is so out of breath that he has to stop. There is a fallen tree trunk close by and he sits down. He wipes the sweat from his forehead with the back of his hand. With irritation he thinks about Bongwe's humorous remark that the exercise will do him good.

In the distance he can hear some boys practicing with their drums. He snorts through his nose, they obviously still need a lot of practice. He tried the drums when he was younger but soon lost interest, nothing compares to the thrill of a hunt. The young men's consistent drumming efforts remind him of an incident many years ago. A group from a neighbouring village came to visit them.

Amongst them there was a small, wiry little man with wispy hair and a round face. Under his arm he carried his most prized possession, his drum.

Around the fire later that evening, he told them that he could extract any emotion from them, by simply playing on his drum. They all laughed at the silly suggestion and with a chuckle told him to prove it.

Rhythmic sounds began to fill the air and intrigued with the beautiful sounds he was creating, they watched his supple and sinewy hands. They all felt happy and joyful. They laughed and some people even started dancing. The drummer subtly increased the rhythm and their happiness amplified. It rose higher and higher and even the stolid head warrior smiled and laughed at their high spirits.

With a frown Thukani also remembers what happened when the drummer changed the rhythm. He did it so unobtrusively and smoothly they hardly noticed it. People stopped dancing and sat down again. Smiles disappeared and irritation surfaced. The longer the drummer beat his drum, the angrier and darker their emotions became. It intensified so quickly, that it escalated into a brawl that revealed little sensibility. Even the quick-tongued charmer of the village became a raving lunatic.

Suddenly the drummer stopped and silence hanged in the air. Angry emotions drained from them as quickly as it came. They looked at each other with shock. What exactly had this man just done to them?

The elders were dismayed. Surely there must be some dark forces at work here? Without hesitation they asked him to leave the village immediately.

The drummer was indignant to say the least. "All I wanted to do was show you how powerful the drum can be in the hands of the right player," he said in a high voice. "It's not my fault all states of mind reproduce themselves." He picked up his drum, tucked it under his arm and walked away. They never saw him again.

Thukani shakes his head to clear his thoughts. There are more important things to think about at the moment. He stays on the fallen tree truck till the sun is nearly directly above him. Slowly he gets up and starts limping home in the scorching hot sun.

At the hut he immediately summons Sibongile. His leg is hurting from the long walk and he is irritated that he has to wait for her. When she arrives he notices for the first time how well dressed, graceful, and slender she is.

He gestures to her to sit down beside him and she does so. Her eyes, almost identical to her father's, scan his face. He clears his throat but struggles to find the right words. He has to suppress the rising thought that she is a woman. Right now he needs to hold on to the vision he has for his people. He puts his hand on her arm and says. "My daughter you must be like a rhinoceros. Your skin must be so thick that nothing anyone ever says can penetrate it to hurt you."

Sibongile is used to her father's sometimes-strange ways but she has no idea where this conversation is heading. She gives her father a nervous glance. She saw a huge rhinoceros with a massive body and short, thick legs this morning. His skin was grey and thick and he had two meridian horns, which he uses mostly for defence, on his snout. She knows that the rhinoceros has poor eyesight but she finished her washing as fast as she could.

She sucks in her breath with shock when her father says. "I want you to take over from me as chief." She jumps up and croaks. "Father! You forget that I am a woman!"

"I am well aware of the fact that you're a woman!" Thukani snaps. "Now sit down! I have no intention of looking up at you!"

Sibongile sits down again and folds her hands in her lap to hide her shaking fingers. She knows Mandla suggested she takes over from her father, but never, not even in her wildest dreams, did she think he would consider it.

"The rhinoceros has poor vision, but this deficiency is compensated by an acute sense of smell and hearing," Thukani says. "It is the same with women. They are usually peaceful and timid, but they also have an overwhelming passion to protect their people. A threatened rhinoceros is very dangerous but a threatened woman is even more dangerous!" He snorts through his nose. "I've had the misfortune to clash with a female warrior once and she gave me a limp that I will carry with me till the day I die." He puts his hand on Sibongile's leg. "Take up this task my daughter. It is my wish."

Sibongile returns her father's intent look without flinching, even though butterflies are swirling in her stomach. She hesitates for only a brief moment and says in a low voice. "If it is your will father, I accept."

Thukani nods his head. "Now leave me alone!" he grunts, "I have things to do!"

Sibongile gets up and walks away with a small smile playing on her lips. She never expected her father to bestow such a big honour on her. She lifts her head and pulls her shoulders back. Could she do it? Indeed she can!

Thukani watches her leave. There is no arrogance in the graceful swing on her hips, only strength and determination. Long ago all he cared about were words and traditions. So much that he forgot about his feelings. He won't make the same mistake again. He grins. "Isilwane is back. The Ndebele people will stand proud and strong once more under the leadership of Sibongile!

When darkness falls the Spirit People come out again. They giggle in the moonlight. Many of the young men in the village watches Sibongile's sensuous hip sway and want to kiss her beguiling mouth. She has a passionate energy that makes men groan with anticipation.

Not that it matters. No! Not at all! There are greater things in store for the lovely Sibongile. She is like a line drawing waiting to be animated with colour. They imitate Sibongile by pulling their shoulders back and lifting their heads.

A single start shoots across the horizon. It trails behind it a bright purple and silver line. The moon winks and gurgles with laughter. The possibilities are endless!

Mandla is on his way back to Mthisa. He is retracing the steps that led to so many life-changing experiences for him. He realizes that he doesn't have all the answers yet, but the truth that he has discovered, is comforting and inspiring. He needs to spread his own ray of light as far and wide as he can.

Then one day, at long last, he is back where he started, in front of Mthisa's hut. Neglect and old age hangs like a weary cloak around the hut. The bright, intricate and geometrical painted patterns on the hut are faded and dull. Between the weeds that have taken over the usual clean courtyard, there is a silent sadness.

Mandla swallows hard with guilt and an uncomfortable fear clutches at his heart. He has been gone for a very long time. He calls at the door but only silence greets his request. He clears his throat and calls again, louder this time. When there is no answer he enters. His eyes struggle to adjust to the darkness and he trips over a pile of dry wood that had fallen over.

Mthisa, who had been resting on a woven mat, sits up and peers in the direction of the noise. "Who's there?" she calls out sharply.

Mandla breathes a sigh of relief. She'll never know how welcome her sharp, high voice sounds right now. He walks over to her and kneels beside her. His heart turns over in his chest when he notices her wrinkled face and bony hands. He touches her cheek tenderly and says. "It is I mother, Mandla, I have come home."

Mthisa squints her eyes to take a better look at him. "Mandla is that you?" she asks and before he could even answer, she busts into uncontrollable sobs. He pulls her weak and frail body into a loving embrace while she moans like a little child. "Mandla, oh my Mandla, you've come home………." Mandla closes his eyes and whispers a silent prayer of thanks. Nothing could ever destroy the love they have for each other.

When she starts disentangling herself, he lets her go. A bit out of breath she struggles to get up and when he tries to help her, she shakes off his hand. "I'm not totally useless, you know!" she says irritably. She takes her walking stick and orders, "Come outside, I can see better in the sunlight."

Outside they sit down on some old faded wooden chairs underneath a big sausage tree. A light wind rustles the sausage-like pods hanging in the tree.

Mthisa's scans his face with eyes that, even though impaired, are still eagle sharp. His face has lost its youthful, innocent look, and he is definitely not the same confused young man that left home what seems to be so very long ago. She slowly nods her head when she notices the white streak in his long hair. That only happens when you have a powerful spiritual experience. That is why he now has an aura of power around him and his eyes look as if they know some hidden secret. "I want to hear everything," she says in a high voice barely able to contain her excitement. "You are to tell me everything! Leave nothing out, you hear! However unimportant you might think it is. I want to hear everything!

Mandla grins, her body might be old and weak but there's nothing wrong with her mind. He pretends to cough. "I don't think I'll be able to talk till I've had something to drink," he teases her. "My throat feels like sage scorched dry by the sun."

Mthisa gives a loud snort. "Well then, don't stand around," she snaps. "Get some beer. There's nothing wrong with your hands I hope!"

Mandla gets up and roars with laughter. It's good to be home! When he returns she is fiddling with her clothes trying to hide her impatience. He hands her a calabash filled with corn bear and winks at her as she takes it. He grins when she clicks her tongue and frowns at him.

For a while they drink their beer without taking. They both know that Mandla's thoughts have to go back in time, and that he has to work through the series of events that brought him to the present moment. When he starts talking his first words are scattered, but it as time passes, it takes form, and he tells her all the fascinating events of a journey that created its own momentum.

The sun's shadows have already begun to lengthen and stretch when Mandla stops talking. He looks at Mthisa and sees the exhaustion on her face. "We can talk some more tomorrow," he says to her, "I think you should rest now."

Mthisa nods her head. Her body is aching from sitting still for so long, but she ignores the pain as she always does. She takes a deep breath and reaches for her walking stick. "You have changed," she says to Mandla.

"Yes I have," Mandla answers. "Change is life."

"Wise words," Mthisa says with a nod.

Mandla smiles. "Everything I am is because of you my mother. You are the greatest gift I ever received."

Mthisa jerks her head up and her eyes flash. "Don't say that! Every one you meet comes to you with a gift in their hands. All you have to do is put out your hand and take it."

Mandla chuckles. "Even now you are still teaching me."

"One is never too old to learn," Mthisa grunts. "I'd have thought that you would know that by now."

Mandla takes her arm and they slowly walk back to the hut. He helps her to lie down and she does so with relief. She is still busy shifting around to find a comfortable position for her aching body when she hears the lonesome drawn out call of a fish eagle. A small smile plays on her lips. She is ready to let go of earth life. She has been ready for a long time.

The fish eagle shatters the stillness once more with his call before he stretches his wings and swoops down to Mthisa. The Spirit People help him lift her out of her old worn out body and puts her onto his wings. Mthisa stretches her arms and laughs. She is filled with joy and freedom. Her life is good, so very good. She looks down on her beloved Mandla once more then speeds away on swift wings to the space beyond time and limits.

The Spirit People stay with Mandla while he is in the warm comfort of the sleep world. With feather light fingers they touch him. From the beginning, they shared each and every moment with him. Their soft cries would join him in moments of pain and their tears would splatter on the moonbeams like silver raindrops. They also experienced his joyful exhilaration in magical moments. Then they would smile, giggle and dance with the joy of life.

Tonight they won't dance on the moonbeams. They want to stay here, close to Mandla. So much has happened since the beginning. When was it again? Yesterday? A lifetime ago? They give a sigh and a light wind blows through the hut. It makes no difference. All that is important is the here and now.

Chapter 20
I Am Everything That Is

Mandla stays in the village till after Mthisa's burial. He makes sure she gets buried next to her best friend Zinhle. Zinhle died about a year ago and she was the only person whose company Mthisa tolerated, possibly because of everything they had to endure to get their children to safety. Mthisa still preferred to be alone.

On Mandla's last night, in Mthisa's now dilapidated hut, he goes outside and looks at the first evening star that sparkles in the darkening sky. Later others will join it, but for now it is content to shine alone. It reminds him of Mthisa. He will try his best not to mourn her. Intuitively he knows she will always be with him.

Early the next morning, just as the sun starts peeking over the horizon, he sets fire to Mthisa's hut. Because of the dry grass, which serves as a roof for the hut, the flames spread quickly. While the thick smoke spirals upwards and the flames grow and lick at the dry wood, Mandla turns and walks away. There is nothing here of value to him anymore.

Villagers wearily watch the burning hut. Surely Mandla knows that the fire can spread and endanger their homes! They frown at him when he walks past them out of the village. Just as well he is leaving, he is as strange as Mthisa!

Mandla is fully aware of the angry stares, but it doesn't bother him. When he left the village, what seems to be so long ago, it was one of the most difficult things he had ever done in his life. Then he thought he was content gathering and mixing herbs, but now it seems to be so insignificant. He nods his head as he steadily walks on. When something no longer serves us, we move away from it and change.

When he gets to the river he bends down to scoop some of the clear, pure and crisp water in his hand to quench his thirst. As usual the sun is scorching hot. The cool liquid slips delightfully down his throat. He starts to fill his calabash but keeps his eyes on a herd of hippopotamus close by.

All that is visible above the surface of the water is their eyes, ears and nostrils. Their heavy, short legged and short tailed bodies are hidden beneath the water. A large male, protecting the herd, moves closer to the river's edge when he sees Mandla. He snorts with his nostrils, which are surrounded by sparse, bristly hairs and equipped with special flaps that close down when he goes under water. He opens his huge mouth as wide as he can to reveal his dangerous pointed incisor and canine teeth.

Mandla can't control the shiver the runs down his spine. The aggressive male reminds him of the disgusting whip Matsisi had made out of hippopotamus hide. He shakes his shoulder to lose the feeling and starts walking downstream. The huge hippopotamus male swims alongside. His distrustful nature will not rest until he can't see and smell Mandla anymore.

With a degree of discomfort Mandla keeps his eyes on him. It is the same feeling he sometimes had when he was around Matsisi. He looks up at the sky as if he is talking to his brother. "I hope you are at peace now Matsisi," he says to the clear blue sky. "I hope your anger, pain and bitterness has left you and that you have become whole. Like the hippopotamus, which can live inside and outside the water, I hope you have learned that there is a physical and a spiritual side to our lives, and that the one cannot exist without the other." He gives a deep sigh and his heart aches. How he wishes that things could have been different between him and his brother. He shakes his head and continues walking. He has learned the secret of life is not to have everything you want, but to want everything you have.

There is a sharp left curve in the river. It causes a build up of water that crashes with relentless force on the rocks obscuring their pathway. It pounds and splashes and through the ages of time, it will eventually remove the big boulders trying to stop the even and smooth flow of the water. Nothing remains the same. It is the law of life.

Mandla doesn't follow the swerving river. Instead he walks straight ahead in an easterly direction. He doesn't really know where he is going and neither does he worry about it. All he knows, without a doubt, is that he must walk in the direction of the rising sun where all days are born.

Mandla journey east is without incident and he becomes a bit irritated because nothing is happening. He needs to hunt for some food as he had used the last of his supplies this morning. As luck would have it there is an eland right in front of him. It has a fawn-coloured coat with a broad, deep-fringed dewlap and strong horns spiralling straight upwards. His nose is lifted high in the air and his body tense and uncomfortable.

Mandla is still watching the eland when a cheetah, disguised in the bushes with her yellow-brown coat and black spots charges the eland. He tries to move away but it feels as if his legs are rooted to the ground. Mandla sucks in his breath and keeps as still as he can. As he watches the cheetah with wide eyes, his birthmark starts burning and there is a pulling sensation in the centre of his forehead. A bright flash blinds him for a moment and when he recovers, he feels as if he is one with the cheetah.

Without any communication he knows that she must make a kill today as her cubs, with their long, silky grey mantles over the back of their heads, are ravishingly hungry. The feelings of the cheetah become his feelings. He feels his own muscles contract in harmony with hers, and the breath rushing through her lungs becomes his own.

She digs her claws, which cannot retract, into the ground. Her body, adapted to running rather than for leaping from an ambush, flash through the air. She feels the hot wind sweep over her body and the ground move beneath her feet. She feels exhilaration course through her sleek body with the pure joy of being alive. She contracts her muscles to run even faster and relishes the moment in the knowledge that she can run faster than anything she knows.

Mandla has become one with the drama of life that unfolds before him. When she drags the eland away to feed her cubs the connection breaks. Mandla sinks to the ground and sits down. He feels like he has been holding his breath all the time and his legs like they don't want to carry him anymore. He stares at the empty space where the cheetah was a moment ago. How is it possible that he could connect to the cheetah at that level?

Though the experience was quite amazing Mandla still has no understanding of why it happened. Eventually he gives up trying to make sense of it. He continues heading east and leaves the dry and open grassland. Ahead of him, in a blue-grey haze towers a mountain range. He reaches it sooner than he expected and sets up camp in a protected spot. While eating he looks at the large peeks reaching up into the sky and gives a deep sigh. He really doesn't feel like the big climb ahead of him tomorrow.

Early the next morning Mandla start climbing, the quicker he gets this over with, the better. When he reaches the first high peak he is out of breath. He sits down to rest and drinks some water from his calabash. After awhile he gets up and starts climbing again. He feels a bit lightheaded but ignores it. He wants to get as high as he can before nightfall.

It is already late afternoon when he stops climbing. He will have to camp here for the night, as there is not enough daylight left to start the next treacherous climb. He shivers when an icy cold wind cuts into him. He unrolls his colourful blanket and pulls it across his shoulders. He needs to look for firewood but just doesn't have the energy. Besides that, his light-headedness has increased considerably. He pulls the blanket even closer around him. He doesn't know if he is just exhausted from the long climb or simply just too cold.

On the horizon the sun begins to lower itself. It paints the sky in red, purple and orange colours infused between the clouds. The moon also appears in the sky and its dim glow begins to brighten. It is not day, and neither is it night.

Mandla mumbles under his breath when his birthmark starts burning. He pulls back the soft impala skin and notices with surprise that the triangle has taken on a luminous violet glow. He drops the impala skin when the pulling sensation in the centre of his forehead becomes so strong, that he feels he wants to faint with the force of it. With eyes that are slightly out of focus he looks at the horizon. It seems as if the setting sun and rising moon are moving closer to him. He shakes his head and rubs his eyes. Surely it's not possible?

They continue to move closer to Mandla and after a while they are so close he feels as if he could actually touch them! With eyes that are wide with wonder he tentatively puts out his hand. The blanket slips off his shoulder but he doesn't notice, neither does he feel the icy wind or cold anymore. His whole being is focused on what is happening and with every moment that passes, he becomes more and more immerged in it.

The sun and moon has stopped the flow of their cycles. They allow the state of neither day nor night to continue. They turn to each other, combine their powers and merge. As they do so, they form a third identity. They call themselves MoonSun. MoonSun moves closer to Mandla's outstretched hand. Once they connect they will pull him into the very core of their being.

Mandla feels the energy as they connect. He loses all awareness of his body and becomes nothing more than a strand of energy stretching towards MoonSun. This strand of energy contains everything that he is.

There is an explosion of pure joy when they connect. MoonSun and Mandla feel it at the same time. They merge and a fourth identity is born. They will call themselves MoonSunMandla. MoonSunMandla becomes its own strand of energy, one that is part of the whole universe. It darts across the sky with the speed of light. It splashes in vast expansions of water and penetrates the invisible realms of the Spirit World. It feels the essence of God and connects to the universal current of life.

MoonSunMandla shouts with joy. "God is in everything! He is in every strand of energy in the universe and I am part thereof. I am part of everything that is, therefore I am also everything that is!" MoonSunMandla's perception has changed, and time has lost its relevance as if it has never existed at all. It is only concerned with the process of experiencing itself anew in every moment. It is totally and completely immersed in the wonder of I am, I am, I am.

The sun is already high in the sky when Mandla wakes up with a jerk. A bit confused he looks around and it takes him a while to realize where he is. He shakes his head at the intense experience he had. He tries to remember when the experience stopped or when he went to sleep, but he can't. He gets up and stares at the horizon. "So Mthisa was right, you can connect to any part of the whole and when you do, you know without a doubt that you are one with God."

He grins and starts gathering his things. Soon he is climbing again. "At long last I understand why you cannot learn from the experiences of others but only your own," he thinks. "Not only do I now know who and what I am, but more importantly, what I want to be." As he navigates his way over the mountain his heart sings. "I want to bring joy where there is sadness and peace where there is anger. Most of all where there is hatred I want to bring love. I want to give everyone the same gift I received. The gift of love!"

As he crosses over the highest point of the mountain range he can see the lush green countryside below him. Several thin whips of smoke spiral up between the trees. As he starts his slow decent he wonders what awaits him between the tall and majestic trees below.

As the sun finished setting the moon begins to create the night, a million stars starts to twinkle in the deep purple sky. The Spirit People begin to dance on the moonbeams as they have done since the beginning of time. In the village between the majestic trees they sprinkle moon dust all around so everyone can have a good night sleep. Mandla will arrive tomorrow and the villagers will learn that everything is constantly changing, all the time.

They dart over to Mandla who is also fast asleep in a protected crevice on the mountainside. They touch him with feather light fingers and call him "Beloved." They surround him and begin to chant in their strange language. While Mandla is in a deep sleep they are showing him, like they did Mthisa, how to live more deeply in the undistracted centre of his being. Here the will cannot intrude and the sense of time passing will be lost.

They continue to chant and starts calling to the Guardians of the world of form.

We call to the Guardians of the Watchtower of the East where all days are born. You are yellow like the sun and have the power to make things grow.

We call to the Guardians of the Watchtower of the South. You are red hot like the fire. Your energy gives us our blood red life force.

We call to the Guardians of the Watchtower of the West. You are blue like the sky and water. You are tranquil and calm and contain all the wisdom.

We call to the Guardians of the Watchtower of the North. You are black like the night and your darkness has the power to kill.

Be here with us now Guardians!

The Guardians appear. They will keep watch. Mandla is more protected than he will ever know.

And Mandla, the one called Beloved, begins to have a strange dream. He dreams of the birth of a very powerful girl in a place called, "The land of the long white cloud." On her back there is a dapple, a small gleaming white mark in the shape of a triangle. He turns and the blanket slips off his body. His own triangular birthmark glows luminously in the moonlight.

When the first of the sun's ray start creeping over the horizon the Spirit People leave. They have awakened Mandla's mind and heart, now they have to awaken his soul and the idea is fragrant with possibilities.

On the flatlands below the mountain a lion roars. It is so forceful that the ground shakes and the sound vibrates through the air. The King of all Beasts shakes his mane, throws his head back and roars again. Proudly he tosses his head and walks away. After all, did Mandla's awakening not begin with the roar of a lion?

THE END